# WORLDSLIP

## BOOK ONE

# KEYS AND NEEDLES

# MICHELLE NICKOLAISEN

Keys and Needles
Copyright © 2016 by Michelle Nickolaisen

# CHAPTER ONE

I assumed I was alone. Apparently, I was mistaken.

I was picking my way down the narrow alley, the most direct (if not cleanest, safest, or best lit) way home. Lost in thought, I jumped when I heard a slurred voice from what looked like a pile of smelly rags.

"Hey, baby. How ya doin'?" the rags asked.

"Not interested," I replied without breaking stride.

"*Awww*, come on now, sweetheart," the dark figure said, bracing himself against the wall as he stood up from the pile of garbage. He staggered toward me, off kilter. "There's no reason to be like that."

I ignored him as I made my way down the alley, focusing on my destination rather than the smell coming off him in waves. After a few moments, the man stopped pursuing me and instead muttered disagreeably under his breath.

"Hey!" he shouted. "Come back! Think you're too good for me, you stuck-up bitch?"

I had to stop. I *had* to. Before turning around, I took a deep breath. I knew I shouldn't retaliate, but I was so tempted. And he *was* asking for it. Exhaling, I flicked through my mental Rolodex, scanning for a suitably terrifying image. Pebbles skittered across the asphalt as he approached from behind, probably mistaking my anger for fear.

He was now close enough that I could smell the cheap alcohol and lack of personal hygiene. I could almost *taste* the rank musk in the back of my throat. But that was okay, because the closer he was to me, the stronger the effect would be.

I turned around. He smiled in a predatory fashion, like he'd managed to get the upper hand. Obviously, he wasn't clear on the situation at hand. He opened his mouth, no doubt to say something even smarmier than before—then it hit him.

A tall wraithlike figure materialized between us—or he thought one did, anyway. She wore nothing but a black, velvety shadow, a cutout of a cloudless, starless night. Bone-white hands crept out of long, writhing sleeves. And there was something deeply, unsettlingly *wrong* about her face.

Perhaps it was the fact that the skin was a little too smooth, too porcelain. Her unlined face suggested no expression had ever graced it, let alone a smile. Or maybe it was the three blood-red streaks glistening down her cheekbones and nose, or her eyes—miniature black holes which matched her dress, showing depth but no emotion, not even a reflection of the full moon's light.

The man I'd decided to call Hapless Asshole staggered backward. The wraith reached out a skeletal hand and cocked her head, opening her mouth as though to speak. But once it opened wide—in a semimechanical gesture, like she'd never used it before—spiders emerged instead of words.

Hundreds of tiny black spiders poured out of the opened

portal, scuttling down the spirit's alabaster face, disappearing into the eclipse of her pitch-black dress, and reappearing in stark contrast along her outstretched hands. They surged forward in a miniature tidal wave toward Hapless Asshole. She tilted her head farther as a slight rasp escaped her parted lips.

He stepped back so fast he fell, crashing loudly into a trashcan. His worn trousers included a new stain now, and a new smell to go with it. He opened and closed his mouth like a confused fish finding itself in water that didn't *quite* provide enough oxygen. He completely lost it when the specter took a step toward him. Unleashing a guttural scream, he beat a final retreat. He ran toward the opposite end of the alley, toward people and bars and civilization (albeit the dregs of it).

I couldn't help but grin like an idiot. I *knew* the risk of pulling such a prank, but it had just been too juicy to pass up. Plus, it'd be a while before Hapless Asshole would even think about accosting a girl alone in an alley again.

My smile faded as I thought about the rest of the night and the long day ahead of me tomorrow. I sighed and turned back the way I was headed, toward home.

I was awakened the next morning by bright streaks of sunlight across my face and a loud (but perfectly on tune) melody drifting in from the kitchen, needling into my head like rusty nails.

*"Someone's in the kitchen with Dinaaaah . . ."*

Groaning, I rolled out of bed and fished a ratty T-shirt from the laundry pile at the foot of my bed. I staggered into the kitchen, the worn floors creaking underfoot, still rubbing the sleep from my eyes.

"You know, you could wake the dead with your singing," I told Logan.

Logan kept his attention on the stove. "You're just jealous my singing voice is better than yours."

I found a patch of wall to lean on as I watched him stir eggs in a pan. "What's got you in such a great mood, anyway?"

He smiled to himself. "I had an *excellent* take last night. See for yourself." He gestured over his shoulder with the spatula, pointing toward the table. Indeed, strewn across the tabletop were wads of cash and large piles of gold coins.

"Mmm. And how many victims did you have to glamour to get that take?"

"That, dear Tania, was all luck," he said, turning around long enough to give me a wink.

Logan and I have lived together for a few years now. It wasn't like *that*—he wasn't playing on the same team. Or not playing for my team. Whichever way that metaphor goes. Sports were never my strong suit.

We met just after the Slip, when the government hadn't yet figured out what to do with the Marked, aside from quarantining us. The jerk had the gall to critique my glamouring technique, and we became fast friends from there. His primary source of income came from a mixture of gambling and gods know what else. Being full Fae, he could charm himself into and out of any situation. At least, any situation on this side of the Slip.

The money he managed to keep by the end of the month supplemented the tiny monthly stipend the government paid me as compensation for living in a fenced-in slum. Since Logan wasn't human and therefore didn't exist as far as the government was concerned, he got no such stipend. I did my best to add to it, given that I wanted to pay for more than rent and running water. Little things, like food that didn't come in a can, or clothes that didn't come out of a dumpster. That's why I'd been at that stupid bar last night in the first place.

"And how was *your* night?"

"Ugh," I grunted. "No luck at the bar, and I got accosted by some asshat on the way home."

He turned around, leaning against the stove with a smirk on his face, already knowing the answer to the question he was about to ask.

"And how did that turn out for said asshat?"

I grinned. "He pissed himself and ran."

"Titania!" Logan fake-scowled. "Out of bounds, past curfew, *and* you glamoured some drunk into hysteria? Tsk-tsk!"

I rolled my eyes. "Don't call me that. You know I hate it when you use my full name."

Titania—queen of the faeries. My mom was a big mythology and folklore buff. Kind of ironic, considering. Hearing my full name made me think of her, causing a dull ache to burrow in my chest. Of course, Logan wouldn't understand, given that his family ordered his lover killed in front of him. And that was *before* they banished him as punishment for trying to get out of an arranged marriage. No love lost there.

"Still, it is a little reckless, even for you," Logan said. "You're in that neighborhood a lot. If stories got out about a Marked on the loose, accosting poor innocent bystanders, there could be consequences."

I snorted and waved away his worries. "Half the patrons of those bars are doing something illegal. Being out of bounds past curfew is small potatoes for those people."

A flicker of concern crossed his face. "'People' being the operative word there, Tania. I know you don't like the reminder, but you can't ever forget they don't think of you as a person. You're not like them, and they resent you for it. If it came down to turning in a Marked for illegal glamouring or a scumbag drug dealer for breaking into someone's home, you know who they'd go after first. They think it's us versus them."

I heaved a sigh. He was right, of course, but admitting it would make him insufferable for days, genuine concern aside. Time for a change of subject.

"Whatcha cookin' there?" I crossed the room and peered over his shoulder.

"Oh, you know. Just your basic bacon-and-spinach omelet. I figured since I was a big winner last night, we could eat a real breakfast today and then visit the market. I even made enough to share, like the wonderful roommate I am."

I laughed. "Made enough money or omelet?"

He grinned. "Both."

We ate mostly in silence. We've lived together long enough that silence was as comfortable as chit-chat, and I'd run out of things to tease him about. *Visiting the market's a good idea*, I thought. I might not have made any money last night, but I had gotten my stipend the day before and still had a little stashed away. Our fridge looked pretty pitiful at the moment and could use some restocking. The rest of the known world, living in the twenty-first century, didn't have to rely on outdoor markets for all their needs. But our income, even supplemented, didn't allow for luxuries like computers, so online shopping was right out. Not that it'd be easy to get UPS to ship to our part of the city.

Back before the Slip, I'd been pretty tech savvy. I used to love the Internet. Now I missed it. I missed making friends and connections from all over the world. I missed not feeling alone. It didn't seem like a coincidence that we didn't have the means to buy our own tech. It meant we never had a chance to tell our side of the story to the outside world. Or any story other than the latest "Marked Gone Bad!" sensationalism. It was probably a moot point, anyway, since technology tended to go wonky around us and the portals. But it was still unfair and never failed to annoy me.

"You know," I said, setting my fork down and pushing my plate away, "if we go to the market, you're going to have to do something about your looks."

He rolled his eyes. "Don't I always?"

Logan wasn't actually Marked, given that he wasn't from here. You could search him all over and not find a single suspicious birthmark. However, he *was* six feet tall and incredibly good-looking, and had pointy elf ears and naturally green-tinted white-blond hair, which might raise even more suspicion than being Marked. Lucky for him, since he wasn't human, abilities like glamouring and full-blown shapeshifting came as naturally as breathing.

"What about you?" he asked. "Do you think you'll make any tweaks today? I mean, don't get me wrong—I like the purple in your hair, but you could try something new. Hazel eyes might go nicely with the purple."

"Nah. I'm okay with the way I look, for now," I said. "Besides, why get dressed up just for market?"

A few years before I met Logan, I couldn't control the finer points of my powers. I could hardly change anything about my appearance without changing *everything* about it. Great for disguises and the less-than-legal work I picked up. Major annoyance the rest of the time. Years later, after a lot of focused practice, I could now change smaller details like my eye color at a whim.

"What about your clothes?" He glanced at my left arm— the arm with the Mark on it. A dark-brown birthmark shaped like a skeleton key stretched from midway down my inner forearm to the pad of my thumb, its teeth ragged and gnawing at my palm.

"Why bother?" I said. "Nobody goes to the market except us Marked, and it's not like wearing a long-sleeved shirt and fingerless gloves on a sunny day is inconspicuous."

He shrugged. "Okay, suit yourself. Ready in ten?"

An hour later, we were browsing the stalls. The market was a cacophony of sights and smells, everything from strips of roasted meats to fragrant herbs and colorful fruits. The bright produce contrasted with the often rickety-looking stalls, meant to be set up and taken down quickly, and the run-down buildings surrounding the dirt lot.

The offerings were a little picked over. We'd shown up too late in the day. For the best stuff, we would have had to get there at nine or so, but the chances of my being anywhere at 9:00 a.m. on a Saturday were slim to none. We'd bought a few discolored tomatoes and apples, but I still wanted to get eggs. So Logan and I split up, since he wanted to find fresh fruit (which I couldn't afford).

"Tania!" a woman's voice called amid the crowd. It sounded much friendlier than I was used to, which surprised me. I turned. A woman with dark hair and sparkling brown eyes was waving from two stalls down. I walked over to her booth of worn but clean tables housing her wares.

"Hi, Rosa!"

"How are you, cariña? I haven't seen you here in a while. Are you eating enough?" She scanned me up and down disapprovingly, taking in the ratty clothes and overall mess of my appearance.

I laughed. Even if the concern was excessive, it was nice to have someone who wasn't Logan looking after me. It was an especially nice change here; aside from Rosa, most of the sellers treated us Marked with disdain and suspicion. They knew the market was one of the few places in the city where we could shop, and they were only here to make a quick buck off of us. "I'm fine, Rosa. I'm getting enough to eat, working odd jobs here and there . . ."

"Of course. What they pay you isn't enough to cover everything." Rosa shook her head, clucking her tongue and furrowing her eyebrows. "Anything look good here? I'll give you a discount."

Not only did she have the eggs I needed, she also had a loaf of freshly baked bread and a large assortment of potatoes to boot. While I browsed the produce, I noticed a pair of small brown eyes peeking out from behind one of the tables. I crouched down, suppressing a smile. "Who's this?"

Rosa smiled and beckoned for the child to come out. "This is Alejandro, my nephew. He just turned seven and wanted to see what Aunt Rosa does on the weekends. I told him he could come as long as he helped set things up and kept inventory. He's got to earn his keep." She winked at me.

I stuck my hand out. "Hi, Alejandro, I'm Tania."

He shook my hand enthusiastically, any residual hint of shyness disappearing like dew in the sun.

"Are you having fun helping out your Aunt Rosa?"

"Yes. I like watching all the people." He looked at my Mark and, with the boldness only small children can pull off, asked, "Can you do magic?"

Rosa flinched and blushed bright pink. "Alejandro! That is a rude question. I'm sorry, Tania." She grabbed his shoulder to lead him away.

I laughed and placed my hand on her arm. "Rosa, of all the things I hear, a child asking if I can do magic is certainly the least rude. Here, Alejandro, do you want to see a trick?"

He nodded emphatically, jerking his hand away from Rosa and leaning in to watch me, his eyes as round as those gold coins Logan was showing off earlier. Rosa mouthed "Thank you" with an apologetic smile, then slipped away to deal with another customer.

I pulled a quarter out of my pocket. "This is a magic quarter. Do you want to see why?"

He nodded again, quivering with excitement. I tried not to laugh. When I was younger and couldn't control my skills yet, I still had to find a way to cobble together a living. Although I wasn't the best pickpocket around, I knew a few nifty sleight-of-hand tricks. I made a big show of dropping the quarter into my left hand while I hid it in my right. I closed my left hand into a fist, held it out to him, and turned it over to show it was empty, then lifted my right hand to his ear and pulled the quarter out of it. He laughed and clapped his hands, shrieking, "Show me another one! Show me another one!"

I giggled, too, but my laughter was cut short by a horrified "I never!" that sliced through the commotion of the crowd. I glanced around and noticed an older woman who appeared to have been watching my little magic show. She waited until I locked eyes with her and then made a huge show of crossing herself, huffing in disgust. "It's bad enough one of *you* is even here, out in public," she snapped, voice dripping with disdain. "I can't believe you're corrupting this child's mind with your devilry."

I glanced at Alejandro to see how he'd react. Before I could say anything, he puffed up his chest in anger. He stuck his chubby little hands on his hips, stared her straight in the face, and said, "Come on, lady! That wasn't even real magic. Are you *dumb*? My grandpa can do that trick. She was just being nice to me."

The woman looked from his face to mine—contorted in my efforts to suppress my laughter—her mouth agape and face flushed red. She opened her mouth and sucked in a distressing amount of air, then marched toward us. By all appearances, she was preparing to launch into a full-blown tirade on the evils of the Marked and kids' attitudes these days. I stood up and squared my shoulders, instinctively stepping in front of Alejandro and preparing for a fistfight. Usually it didn't come to a brawl with the churchy types, but I could never tell for sure. The line between self-righteous anger and self-righteous violence wasn't thick. I took a deep breath and dropped into a more anchored stance, digging my feet into the dirt, when Rosa stepped between us.

Her exact words were "I'm sorry. Can I help you?" But her tone clearly stated, "Don't push me, or the help you get may come in the form of dismemberment."

The stranger's righteous anger deflated somewhat as she glanced from Rosa with her calm but firm demeanor, to Alejandro and his triumphant face, to me. Finally she said, "I'm fine. But mark my words. Nothing good will come from associating with that . . . creature." She waved a hand in my direction, then turned on her heel and stomped off.

We all exhaled in unison. Alejandro broke the silence with a squeal of laughter, throwing himself at his aunt's legs and hugging them. "Thank you for getting rid of the mean lady!"

"Yes." I smiled to show her how much her intervention meant to me. "Thank you. A lot."

She patted me on the shoulder. "No worries. I think we can all agree that old bag needed to be taken down a peg. Now, what were you looking for, Tania?"

I turned back to her table, but I was still awash in an unpleasant mixture of relief and unease. Rosa didn't *have* to stick up for me; we were friendly acquaintances who saw each other a few times a month. But if she hadn't, things could have gotten nasty. I was grateful for her intervention, but the fact that it was even needed in the first place unsettled me. Why was that woman even here? This market was specifically for the Marked, so she was probably looking to give a sermon and just didn't expect to see someone brazenly practicing "magic" in public.

There'd been a rise in holy rollers since the Slip first happened. Fearmongers who took their sacred texts far too literally were inclined to decry the Slip as a sign of the end times—and with it, all the Marked as minions of the Devil. The Slips across the country may have been shuttered away and removed from sight, but we were a daily reminder that something unexplained by their worldview had happened, and they didn't like it. When mysterious tears in reality show up all over the world, and teenagers are randomly bestowed with magical superpowers, it's going to shake some people up.

Anyway, the whole situation created women like Mrs. No-Magic-for-You, willing to use any opportunity to get on a soapbox. The *really* unpleasant types, which weren't all that many in number (but were more numerous than I'd like), were of the opinion the Marked should all be done away with. Their sermons tended to stop there and left it to the listener's imagination to fill in the blanks on how that would happen exactly.

Before I left Rosa's tent, I knelt down on one knee and beckoned to Alejandro. I could get myself in trouble here, but I couldn't resist the idea, given his endearing bravery in the face of bigotry. I leaned over and whispered in his ear, "Do you want to see *real* magic?"

He nodded, his eyes wide. I leaned back so we were still close, but not nearly touching noses. I closed my eyes for a moment, then opened them. They were now a brilliant royal purple with shimmering gold flecks around the irises.

Alejandro let out a small gasp, then smiled with heart-breaking sincerity. He reached out a finger as if to touch my eyes, but instead brushed my cheek. "They're so pretty," he whispered. I smiled at him and blinked, reverting them to their normal shade of blue. He hugged me and said, quite serious, "Thank you, Miss Tania. I know that was special."

Unexpectedly touched by his gratitude and unflinching acceptance, I found myself welling up as I hugged him back. "You're welcome, little guy. Thanks for sticking up for me."

A familiar voice calling from the crowd broke off our exchange.

"Hey, Tania! You about ready?" Logan walked up in his guise of "normal" (but still preternaturally handsome) human with rounded ears and dark hair pulled back in a ponytail. Clearly, he'd had a better time than I did—I noticed several shiny apples peeking from his bags, threatening to burst open the seams.

I coughed and brushed away a stray tear that slid down the bridge of my nose. "Yeah, I think we're good here." Rosa was busy with another customer. I waved in her general direction, then looked at Alejandro. "It was nice meeting you. Maybe I'll see you again another time," I said as I patted him on the head, struck by the contrast between the hate-filled woman and the sweet little boy.

# CHAPTER TWO

t was dark. And I was cold.

Where the hell was I and how did I get here? Above me shone an impossibly large full moon on a black canvas spotted with stars and clouds. A soft hooting sounded in the distance. Behind me were trees—but not like trees in the city. These were three times as wide as me and stretched far, far above my head. I hadn't seen anything rivaling their scale since my mom took me to a redwood forest when I was eight. I still remember touching the trees and trying to believe they were real, their scale seeming impossible to my child's mind.

I looked out over the lake, its glassy surface reflecting the bright moon. The ground under my bare feet was covered in snow, but though I was chilly, I wasn't freezing. I took a few experimental steps forward and noticed I didn't leave behind any footprints in the smooth white powder. I could feel my steps, but in a vague sort of way, as though my sense of touch had been dialed down. Curious, I picked up a twig and bent it, finding that I could indeed snap it in half and hear it. I wasn't entirely formless, I just wasn't . . . all there.

"Okay, we're in some pretty weird territory here," I muttered to myself. "Maybe I'm in a lucid dream?" I'd had them before, though usually in more mundane settings (where I used my lucidity to fly around the room, of course).

I turned back around and faced the forest, figuring that it was as good a place to start as any. Shrugging, I walked toward the tree line and shivered when the owl hooted again, no doubt searching for its dinner. I wished I knew more about nature—growing up in the city hadn't prepared me for suddenly being stuck out in the middle of the forest. Some of the trees were clearly evergreens, but others were without leaves. All were huge, their bark laced with cracks so big I could fit my hand in them. I walked a few hundred feet into the woods and then took note of my surroundings. The trees went as far as I could see in every direction, and the forest just got darker the farther I went. As the owl hooted again, I heard something shuffle deeper in the forest. It sounded big. It occurred to me that without footprints I'd have no way to retrace my steps to the lake.

I turned on my heels and meandered back to the lake. I wondered why it wasn't frozen. It was beautiful under the soft glow of the frost-colored moon. Growing up in the city, I wasn't used to seeing nature at its finest, but at that moment, as the lake shone with the brilliance of a million diamonds, it was captivating.

My moment of awe was cut short when I sensed movement out of the corner of my eye. I whirled around, ready for a confrontation with whatever predator had taken an interest in me. Instead, I was met by a regal white stag coming to drink from the water. My quick turn had startled it and it froze, its dark, liquid eyes locked on mine. We stared at each other for what seemed like hours. I took a careful step back, signaling that I wasn't a threat. It approached the water about fifteen feet from me. Bending its head, it drank from the lake, the ensuing ripples destroying the mirrored surface. Now that we had some breathing room, I scrutinized the creature. It had to be at least six feet tall at its shoulders, and its antlers were as thick as my wrist. It was more like a moose than a deer, though I'd never seen anything like it. And its antlers were actually gold, though maybe that was a trick of the eyes in the moonlight.

Something snagged my attention away from the animal. The ripples on the lake were now met with other larger ones. They appeared to come from the center, but with no visible source. I stepped closer to the edge of the water, the shallow waves lapping against my toes. Out of the corner of my eye, I saw that the enormous stag appeared to have sated his thirst and was staring straight at me. It could have been my imagination, but it seemed like he inclined his head in a small bow before ambling back into the forest.

The ripples were growing larger. A rush of water streamed from their center, after which a woman's head emerged, followed by her body. Her back was to me, but she was wearing a hooded dark cloak that brushed the water's surface. The woman, now standing steady atop the still water, shrugged and then rolled her head, as if stretching out her neck from sitting too long. She took a few steps toward the far side of the lake, and I noticed she was carrying someone. A small sleeping someone. I *hoped* they were sleeping.

The whole spectacle was giving me the willies. I stepped back, wondering if maybe I was better off facing whatever lurked in the dark forest. The woman froze and my heartbeat quickened. Did I make a noise? Did she hear me? Shit, shit, *shit*. Years of street living had honed my survival skills, and I knew when I was in trouble—like now. Every last one of my instincts screamed at me to run as fast and as far as I could. My nostrils flared as I forced myself to breathe slower and try to stay still. My pulse thundered in my ears as the woman turned around. Lacking options, I squeezed my eyes shut, hoping against hope that this was a dream. Or if it wasn't, at least maybe I'd be somewhere else when I opened them.

I sensed, rather than saw, a change in my surroundings. Peeking out of one eye, I realized I was sitting on a bed. I knew this bed. This was my childhood bedroom, with posters of boy bands littering the walls and the plush comforter with the god-awful floral pattern printed in eye-searing colors. Why had I ever thought that was a good idea?

Through the cracked door, I could hear . . . my mom? Oh no. I remembered this moment. This was a scene stolen from my past. If I was right, then what came next was . . .

"No, I'm telling you, Sam, nobody's talking about it on the news, but something weird is going on. My friend's daughter is doing strange things. Her eye color keeps changing, and her hair has started changing color now, too. Tania has the same odd birthmark she does . . . Yeah, I know it sounds crazy, but Tania's been doing weird things lately, too. I don't know what's wrong, but I know something's up. I'm scared. I'm thinking about taking her to a doctor, but I don't know what they'll do. Nobody is talking about this. But I'm telling you. It's real."

This was the point when sixteen-year-old me had shut the door, sat on the bed, curled into a ball, and cried. I wanted to be somewhere else. I wanted to be some*one* else. I wished I hadn't told my mom about the dream I'd had—the dream about the car accident that had killed two of my classmates. But it had scared me, too. Didn't anyone care that I was scared? Why did it have to be all about her? And why was she talking to her friends about me like I was some kind of freak of nature? I didn't like what was happening, either.

Earlier that week, I'd stared at the mirror and wished my eyes were the same gorgeous green shade as Jessica's, the girl at school I'd seen my crush flirting with. I'd blinked, and then they *were*, making me shriek at the top of my lungs. My mom came running into the bathroom, thinking I had seen a roach and swearing about the failure of pest control. But instead I just stood there, blood drained from my face. When she asked me what was wrong, I gestured at the mirror wordlessly . . . only to see that my eyes had returned to their normal color.

I tried to make up an explanation she'd believe. I refused to tell her the truth, because I didn't want to see the same look she'd given me when we'd seen the car crash on the news. The same car crash that I'd dreamed about in Technicolor, the dream that had rattled me enough to tell her about it over breakfast. It had happened exactly as I'd dreamed, the same two classmates, the same car, the same location. I'll never forget the look she'd given me, scared of her own daughter, even as she'd struggled to reassure me while I'd sobbed, terrified.

I forced my eyes closed again. I didn't want to relive these memories. This was ancient history, before the Slip. I had enough on my plate right now without revisiting my abandonment issues in a dream. Is that what this was? A dream? Well, I wasn't having any of it. Irritated, I said out loud to the imaginary ceiling, "Okay, that's enough, I'm waking up now."

And then I did. My eyes snapped open, and I sat up, groggy from being torn out of deep sleep and cold sweat beading on my forehead. The moonlight streamed through the window onto my bed, and I ran my hands over my face and through my hair. What the hell was *that*? I hadn't thought about that incident with my mom in years. And a creepy lady coming out of a freaking lake? *That's it,* I told myself. *No more spicy enchiladas before bedtime.*

I swung my legs over the side of the bed and stood up,

shaking off a lingering emotional hangover. The fear, the sadness, the danger . . . whatever. I was wide awake now and not planning on going back to sleep for fear of similar dreams returning. I might as well get some work done.

Rummaging through my laundry pile at the foot of my bed, I pulled out a pair of tattered jeans. They were a little big on me, but they looked fashionably so, at least. A navy shirt, then my favorite leather jacket—one of the few things I owned that I'd paid for (even if at a thrift store). Judging by the chill in my room, fingerless gloves wouldn't look out of place tonight. A handy disguise for my birthmark, they'd make my work much easier. Pulling on a pair of beat-up boots, my outfit was complete.

If I could help it, I didn't want to disturb Logan on my way out. Not an easy feat, given those big elf ears of his. As I snuck out of my bedroom, I glanced down our tiny hallway. His door was open, showcasing an empty bed. I guess we were both working tonight.

I left the apartment and wove my way through the cluttered hallway. Piles of clothes, the occasional broken electronics, and straight-up trash littered the floor. I didn't know why people even bothered smuggling electronics in. Between the Slip nearby and the Marked in the building, they never worked for long. To each their own, I suppose.

I stepped out into the brisk air and took a deep breath. It frosted the back of my throat as I savored the solidness of this reality—no dulled senses here. Not like back at that lake.

I took one of my favorite shortcuts through the dilapidated buildings of our quarantine. Logan and I knew the guards' schedules and could navigate their curfew-enforcement patrols with ease. We also knew where the weakest spots in the fencing were. I glanced around, double-checking I was alone, then lifted the loose piece and ducked under it. I crossed the train tracks and entered the seedy bar district. Not the best hunting grounds, but my shabby clothes wouldn't stick out. And given that it was already around one in the morning, I couldn't get to a better part of town in time to fit a good night's work in.

I studied the bar signs as I passed each one down the row. I'd hit Whiskey Dick's last week and managed to get in a few hours of work there. I should probably avoid it for another week or two. I hadn't been to Cheer Up Charlie's in a while, but my take was so-so the last time I was there. That left Black-thorne Pub, a dark tavern full of loyal barflies. I ducked into an alley and put on my game face. That meant dark-red lips and lots of smudgy eyeliner around wide aquamarine eyes. Work with the grungy clothes, not against them, after all.

I walked in and scanned the room. Everyone looked pretty drunk, which was good. I went up to the bar and ordered a whiskey sour, my favorite cheap drink. When the bartender asked for my ID, I held up a blank white business card I kept in my wallet. What he saw certainly wasn't an actual State of Missouri driver's license stating I was over twenty-one. The Marked weren't allowed driver's licenses, and our real IDs declared our Marked status, complete with notes on restricted access and curfew enforcement.

He nodded at me, and I had a drink in my hand within a minute. I glanced around the room for an unattached person as I sipped on it. I didn't even have to look for a target; one came to me instead. A drunk man with a faux barbed-wire tattoo peeking out above his shirt collar leaned on the bar next to me. I forced my lips into a slight smile as he swayed back and forth while trying to maintain focus on me. Yes, he'd do quite nicely.

"Hey, babe. How're you doing?"

Resisting the urge to roll my eyes, I tossed my head and flirted with him. I wanted to get a read on how scummy he was before I made my move. I didn't love picking pockets as a side gig, but if I was going to do it, I felt a little more validated by sourcing out assholes and avoiding nice people. Lucky for me (not for him), confirmation came soon afterward, when he leaned across the three feet of personal space between us. He slid one hand around my waist and another around my hips, grabbing a handful of ass and pulling me close to him. I held my breath as he slurred several presumptuous suggestions in my ear, which would have gotten him slapped under normal circumstances.

Instead, I turned my head to avoid breathing in the stale alcohol smell. Using our proximity to my advantage, I lifted his wallet from his back pocket and removed the cash from it. Pulling back, I locked eyes with him long enough to get inside his head and brushed a finger along his jaw. I slipped the wallet back into his pocket with my other hand and glamoured him into thinking he was leaving with me. He'd wake up the next morning with no memory of what had happened but convinced he'd had the night of his life—and that he'd spent all his money on drinks for me. The chances of him filing a police report were slim, but there was still no need to take them. These were my hunting grounds, and I didn't want word getting around that they weren't okay places to go.

He left with a swagger and a smile on his face. And so the night went, at least for the two hours remaining until closing time. Every now and then, I'd run into a not-awful guy and we'd have a decent conversation or play a round of pool before I moved on to another target. A girl's gotta eat, after all.

I left with a wallet not quite overflowing but in a much healthier state than before. Especially considering that I'd bought enough food for the following week or so earlier at the market. If I had another good take in the next week, I might be able to put together enough money to replace some of my winter wear. We were nearing the end of fall and much of it was falling apart. Of course, the chances of me having such a take on a weeknight were pretty low. But either way, it was something to aim for.

I wandered through the streets, taking the same path as earlier but moving a little slower. If I ignored the exhaust-fume/dirty-street smell, it was a gorgeous night, and I wanted to take it in. My jacket kept me warm, and the stars were out in force, with no clouds to mar the view. I glanced up and smiled. My enjoyment was spoiled when my eyes landed on the moon, full and large like the one over the lake. I thought about how the woman rose from the water and the way she moved, full of grace and danger, holding the small limp body.

I shivered. Suddenly, the night was a little too cold for comfort. The rest of the way home—down dirty alleys and under the fence, scraping my knuckles and dodging security guards—I kept my eyes glued to the ground.

# CHAPTER THREE

Later that morning, I staggered into the kitchen. No singing this time to accompany my groggy march from the bedroom—Logan was either still out or in bed. I never kept close tabs on him. He could take care of himself, but it was unusual for him not to be up at this hour. I set a few cups of water to boil and dug out our French press to make coffee.

Ten minutes later, I was sitting at the table with a coffee mug big enough to stick my face in. I sipped its contents carefully, using the moment to detox from the nightmares of last night. I always got a late start on Sunday, since I usually worked well into the night on Saturdays. I hadn't slept particularly well after I'd got in from the bar. No more freaky dreams, just restless, fitful sleep.

If I made sure to get back before curfew kicked in at 6:00 p.m. (early, since it was a Sunday), I could go to a library or bookstore. Maybe I could dig up some information about ladies rising out of lakes and golden-horned stags. I didn't know if I wanted to go down that route, though.

When I was halfway through consuming the small sea of coffee sitting before me, Logan wandered in, yawning and stretching. He was quite the picture. Sleep had ruffled his emerald-tinted hair, and he'd wrapped himself up in a shabby bathrobe that only made it down to midthigh.

"Well, hello there, Sleeping Beauty," I teased.

"We've met. Didn't like her much," he replied. He looked as though he'd have more sarcasm in him, but the carafe of black gold sitting on the counter distracted him. "Oh, you made coffee? Don't mind if I do."

I rolled my eyes. "Of course you don't. So, what kept you up so late last night?"

"Absolutely *riveting* poker game. I couldn't tear myself away, not when I kept cleaning up." He glanced at me, taking in the half-drained mug of coffee and the circles under my eyes. "What about you? You look like you crawled through all nine worlds to get to that coffee."

I snorted. "Thanks. You're too sweet." I rubbed my eyes with the heel of my hand, ridding them of the last remnants of sleep. "I didn't sleep well. I was having bad dreams, so I got up and worked. Tried a pub I hadn't been to in a while. I cleaned up, too. You wouldn't believe the number of drunk douchebags there. Or, since you were at a poker game, maybe you would."

Logan laughed. "Oh, come on. They aren't all *that* bad."

"Mm-hm. Whatever you say." I smiled, raising a skeptical eyebrow. "Anyway, I had a good haul with no incidents, but when I got home, I didn't sleep well then, either. I kinda feel like hell right now."

He cocked an eyebrow. "Bad dreams?" He didn't have to flesh the question out. Both of us knew sometimes my bad dreams turned into bad realities. Logan was good about not being pushy, but if it had been one of those dreams, preparing for the outcome would be better than ignoring it. As we'd both found out firsthand.

I sighed. "Not one of *those* bad dreams. Just . . . upsetting. It felt real, but wasn't. In any case, it was creepy. And then I had a dream about . . . before the Slip. Back at home."

Logan looked a little concerned now but still didn't push; he knew better than to do that. We've been friends for almost four years now. I had mistaken him for a target and tried to trick him. Of course, he'd seen right through my glamour, and then followed me around the rest of the day, critiquing my technique. He'd been getting on my last nerve, and I almost went off at him before he admitted my technique was actually pretty good "for a human." That, in turn, had piqued my curiosity. I'd prodded him until he revealed his lineage. Once we got to know each other a little, we decided we'd be better off working together. I'd show him the ropes of this world, and he'd help me work on my skills as I uncovered them and learned to control them. He'd never admit to it then, but he wasn't used to dealing with humans and wanted some companionship.

In the years since, we've learned more about each other's backstories, bit by bit. But we never pressured each other to share, and we didn't usually get into details or dwell on them. When you're conning strangers for food or digging through the trash for a decent winter coat, you don't want to think about your previous cushy life.

I fixed my eyes on the sludgy remnants of my coffee. "Before the Slip," I repeated, "months before things got really weird. When my powers or whatever appeared. Here and there, one thing at a time. Stupid things. I had a dream about two of my classmates dying in an awful car accident." I blinked back tears, willing myself not to cry. "Their car was T-boned by a truck. They were dead by the time the ambulance got there. It was so realistic, and it tore me up, even though I didn't know the girls that well. I told my mom about it at breakfast, and sure enough, on the news that night we saw it. It had come true, and the look she gave me . . . it was like I wasn't her daughter anymore. From that point on, she was scared of me.

"I hadn't thought about it in a long time. As bad as that was, the things that came later were so much worse. But then last night . . . it was like it was happening all over again. It all came back—the hurt, the fear . . . it was awful." I sniffed and stared out the window.

Logan, who'd been loudly yet somehow thoughtfully slurping his coffee, set his mug down and hugged me around the shoulders. He gave me a quick kiss on top of my head and pulled me out of my seat, spinning me around to look at him.

"Didn't you say you did well last night?"

I started at the change of subject, but I was grateful for it— as he knew I would be. "Yeah, I guess I did. Why?"

"I think that calls for a celebration. Let's go out. Outside the quarantine. We still have almost a solid"—he glanced out the window at the sun—"six hours before curfew. Let's hit up that thrift store you like so much. I know you need new jeans. Maybe we can even go to a real grocery store and get a box of creamer so we don't have to drink our coffee black next time, hmm?" I sniffed away the last of my unshed tears. He squeezed my shoulders one more time before letting go and said, "Last one dressed has to buy the creamer!"

Ten minutes later, we were laughing hard as we fought each other to get out the door first. After a solid minute and a half of tussling, we decided to call it a draw and split the cost of the creamer.

As we made our way down the hall, trading jibes back and forth, I spotted a shadow moving behind the windowpane of the stairwell door. I bit back whatever sarcastic remark I was about to make and held out a hand to get Logan's attention. When he paused, I nodded toward the shadow, motioning that we should be careful. Any kind of violence in broad daylight was unusual, but not so uncommon that we could afford to be careless. I opened the door with a creak and peeked around it, ready for a fight.

"Oh." I exhaled. "Hi, Jake." I drew out the words so I didn't spook him, noticing his even dirtier than usual appearance. "You, uh, doing okay, buddy?"

Jake wasn't quite seventeen and had been on the streets since he was twelve. I tried to give him a helping hand whenever I could. A lot of shady people were willing to prey on young street kids like him, though, and I couldn't offset their influence twenty-four hours a day. Jake had been an off-and-on junkie since thirteen or so. It was a sad, familiar story. Take young kids with pain to dull, fighting for survival on the streets. Add in unethical drug dealers or would-be crime lords who can make ample use of Marked talents. Voila: a recipe for disaster.

Jake took a quick step back, as though he hadn't expected to hear my voice despite my standing three feet in front of him. He scanned me from head to toe and then glared past me at the wall behind us. His dark gaze was intense, like he was trying to spot a treasure map in the dirty, cracked plaster.

"Oh. Hi, Tania. Hi." His words were breathless, staccato. "I'm good, just, you know, hanging out." He glanced at Logan. "Hi, Logan, what's up? I hear you're good at poker. We should play sometime. I'm getting pretty decent."

Logan and I glanced at each other, uncomfortable. He was either on something or coming off it. "We're good, dude. You sure you're okay? Are you getting enough to eat?" I found myself echoing Rosa's words from the day before. I looked him over again, taking in the ratty superhero T-shirt hanging onto his skinny shoulders for dear life and the tattered jeans falling off his bony hips. Being an only child, I'd never had to watch out for someone younger. I was bad at it, never sure when to intervene and when to step back. Jake pulled at my heartstrings and made me willing to risk the awkwardness. Nobody should have to fend for himself at his age. It just wasn't right.

"What? Huh? Yeah, lots of good food. I promise." He ducked his head and half smiled, which just about did me in.

"Okay. Well, you know you're welcome to come over for dinner sometime, if you want." I smiled again and reached out to pat him on the shoulder. He flinched, as though he expected me to hit him. I withdrew my hand and tried to meet his eyes. "If you ever need help . . . if someone is mistreating you or something, we might be able to help."

He glanced in my direction again but didn't hold eye contact. Two jerky nods and then he was through the door. I sighed as I watched him go. When I turned to Logan, he was staring at me with concern.

"Someone is fucking that kid up, Logan. It's not right." I turned away, defensive, and headed down the stairs. He followed.

"I agree. But, Tania, that's scary stuff. You don't want to mess with a drug dealer. Or the person in charge of the drug dealer. And—I hate to say it, because Jake seems like a sweet kid—years of being on that stuff can change you. A person eventually starts to view others as a means to an end. A way to their next score."

A kid junkie once had forcefully tried to get money out of me for his next fix. I hated that Logan was right. "You have a lot of junkies in fairyland?"

He made a face. "I could make some wiseass comment how not all junkies are hooked on drugs. Instead, I'll just remind you that I've been here for five years and encountered my fair share."

"I know, I know, you're right, Logan. But it's not like he could take on either of us, even if he did get the mind to. And I doubt he'll take me up on my offer."

He shrugged, and we finished the trek down the stairs in silence. Since it wasn't past curfew yet, we didn't have to sneak through a hole in the fence. Instead, we went through the main gate, where the guards patted us both down to make sure we weren't carrying weapons. They were *supposed* to check IDs to make sure we were Marked, but they never bothered. Why would a non-Marked person be in our quarantine? The only other people who came here were drug dealers and various unsavory types. Nobody cared much if we wound up dead or addicts until we took it outside our gates. It worked out just as well for us, since Logan didn't have a government-issued ID. If he wanted to, he could glamour the guards into thinking he had one, but he'd never had to. In fact, anyone could—a glaring logistical oversight the guards never addressed. Probably because addressing it would involve admitting to the existence of supernatural powers. Something the government was still averse to, even in the presence of undeniable evidence. Bureaucracy, am I right?

The neighborhoods around the Marked quarantine weren't what you'd call upscale by any means. It never bothered us, because we didn't have any need for nice places. It wasn't like we could afford them.

Our first course of action was to hit up the thrift shop. In short order, I found a pair of jeans and Logan found a jacket. I was quite satisfied with myself until I checked out. Without thinking, I held out my left hand for the change instead of my right. My jacket sleeve slid up, baring my Mark. The cashier practically wet her pants when she saw it. All color drained from her face, and her hands shook, scattering the change on the counter.

I scrunched my nose in annoyance as she scurried away, making an excuse about how she was due for her lunch break. A few aisles down, she grabbed another employee's sleeve and pointed at me in distress. The customers behind me were now craning their necks, wanting to see what was causing the hold-up. The other employee had shaken off the cashier and was heading my way. Aiming to avoid a scene, I scooped up my change and headed out the door.

The law said we were allowed in stores during noncurfew hours. That didn't mean anyone had to be happy about it or couldn't find another reason to kick us out. I ducked into an alleyway and watched the door for Logan. He exited a few minutes later, laughing and waving good-bye to the employee, who suspiciously glanced down the street before shutting the shop door.

"Over here, Logan." I waved an arm from the alley.

"What's up with lurking in alleys, Tania? I've told you before, dark and mysterious isn't your thing."

"Yeah, I made a rookie mistake. Checking out and . . . " I stuck out my arm to demonstrate, rolling my eyes. Wearing gloves would have prevented this whole debacle, but I couldn't do that if the weather wasn't "of an appropriate temperature," or it could be counted as an attempted covering of the Mark.

"Ooohh." He made an annoyed clicking sound with his tongue.

"No big deal, I guess. I still got a pair of jeans that are in better shape than half my wardrobe and fit well for, like, ten bucks. I'll just be careful the rest of the day."

We resumed our shopping. Leery of causing another incident, I gave him my half of the money for the creamer so he could go to the grocery store alone. Logan, not being Marked and having charm oozing out his ears, never had to worry about such things. That, and glamouring took so little effort for him. If anyone asked to see his ID, he could wave them away with less effort than it took me.

As we headed home, I saw a sign for a store I hadn't noticed before. "Used Books and Recycled Reads" the sign proclaimed in faded navy-blue letters.

"Hey, Logan. Wait a sec."

He glanced at the sign, then shrugged. "I think I've still got a few bucks left. Maybe I can find a Western I haven't read yet." (Logan, being from another world, found Westerns endlessly fascinating.)

We were greeted by the comforting smell of old books. Judging by the handwritten signs, one side of the store was nonfiction and the other was fiction. Books were crammed into every available inch of space: on tables, shelves, and even neatly stacked on the floor. The shelves stretched far over my head, almost to the tall ceiling, and could be reached using rolling ladders.

Logan made a beeline for fiction and methodically searched the stacks for his favorite authors. I wandered around with less purpose, wondering if there was someone to help me find what I needed. After navigating an endless maze of shelves, I found a desk with a small balding man behind it, large glasses perched on his hooked nose.

"Excuse me, sir."

He peered up at me, his eyes magnified by the thick lenses. I could see every line of color in his irises. Finding myself a little put off by the effect and still rattled from earlier, I stuttered, "Um . . . where are your books on fairy tales and mythology?"

He leaned back in his chair, which gave a loud squeak of protest, and drummed his fingers on his stomach, which strained to escape the stained gray sweater vest. Pointing to the end of the desk, he finally replied, "Well, we have an electronic catalog. You can search it if you're looking for something specific."

I spared the computer a nervous look. It already appeared to be on its last legs, and I felt sure it was older than me. I didn't want to risk literal sparks flying and destroy this poor shopkeeper's electronics on accident.

"I'm, um, I'm actually not too great with computers. And I'm not looking for anything specific. Can you just point me in the right direction?"

He gave me another once-over, lowering his glasses to peer at me over the top of them. "Sure, I guess. I dunno how a kid like you winds up not being able to use a computer. Seems like all kids nowadays are pretty much born on 'em."

I fidgeted, sure this was about to take a turn for the worse. But he continued without pressing the matter.

He pointed to my left, to another side room I hadn't even noticed. "Just head down to the end of that shelf and swing around the edge of World History. The Folklore and Mythology section is right after World Religions." He laughed, as though he'd made a joke. "I mean, they're pretty much all the same thing these days, anyway, right?"

I forced a laugh and thanked him. I took care to keep my pace measured and calm, not wanting to seem nervous, and heaved a sigh of relief once I was out of sight. I thought he was going to get nosy about why I didn't like computers, with a maybe disastrous outcome. One near-scene in a day was enough for me, thank you. Safe in the stacks, I skimmed the shelves. A title caught my eye: *Encyclopedia of Mythology and Symbols Around the World*. That seemed like a decent enough place to start.

I grunted, heaving the massive tome off the shelf, hooked my foot around a nearby stepstool to pull it over, and sat down. Flipping through to the index, I ran a finger down the *S* column. There it was: "Stag, White: 653." I flipped to the page and skimmed the article. Eventually, I found the subheading for "White Stag" and read in earnest.

"White deer hold a place in the mythology of many cultures. The Celtic people considered them to be messengers from the otherworld, but they also played an important role in other pre-Indo-European cultures, especially in the north. The Celts believed that the white stag would appear when one was transgressing a taboo, such as when Pwyll trespassed into Arawn's hunting grounds."

No golden antlers, but still interesting. The cloaked lady *did* seem like she was up to no good. Or maybe it was all a message from my subconscious to commit fewer taboos. I snorted at that thought and then flipped back to the index, looking for "Lake."

Before I found anything, I heard a noise behind me. I slammed the book shut, stood up, and whirled around, heart pounding, already in fight-or-flight mode. Logan was holding an armful of beat-up Westerns and trying not to giggle.

"I mean, you don't have to fight me for these. I'd be happy to let you borrow them after I'm done."

I relaxed. "Sorry. Just . . . jumpy. I thought the clerk was going to start asking awkward questions."

His eyes fell on the book I'd dropped on the stepstool. "Why are you reading an encyclopedia on mythology and folklore?"

I shrugged and tried not to sound defensive. "Just curious. About a few things. Nothing important." He looked skeptical and attempted to meet my eyes. I fixed my gaze on his stack of books in an attempt to change the subject. "Find some good stuff?"

Logan wasn't done with his line of questioning, I could tell. But he allowed me to distract him, regaling me with the tale of how he'd found books that he hadn't read yet from all his favorite authors.

"And," he continued as he paid the clerk and we left the store, "don't think you got away with that weirdness back there. You're definitely telling me about it later. Something's up with you, and I won't rest until I find out what. One could say it's my sacred duty as a roommate." He flung his hand over his heart and looked heavenward.

I poked his side, and his mouth twitched at the corners. "Whatever. Maybe I'm working on getting better at that whole mysterious thing."

He seemed content to drop the subject for now, although I knew he'd bring it up again later. We made our way back through the streets in the orange light of the sunset. Our return *just* before curfew earned us a snotty comment from one of the guards about how we needed to watch our step.

Back at our building, Jake was nowhere to be found. I couldn't help but hope he was doing a little better than earlier. He'd tried to stay clean before but always backslid. It was no small wonder, with no support system and all.

I helped Logan cook dinner and we cleaned up afterward. We retreated to our rooms, silently settling into the end of the day. He was probably already lost in a Western, but my mind was filled with a restless unease. I stared out the window, thinking about the dream lake. Sleep soon snuck up on me and I dozed off, wrapped up in blankets, my face resting on the windowsill.

# CHAPTER FOUR

Seriously, I was back here *again*?

I heaved a sigh as I surveyed my surroundings, checking to see if I was where I thought I was. Massive full moon, check. Thick snow that I wasn't leaving footprints in, check. Cold outside, distressingly dark forest, and glass-like lake. Check, check, and check. I didn't see the stag anywhere, but he was the only thing missing. I tried to get my bearings, which was difficult without any big landmarks. If I was remembering right, I was even in the same spot I had wound up in before. Was this a new recurring dream? But no . . . My clothes were different, the same ones I'd fallen asleep in.

I knew that venturing into the woods was a bad idea. No footprints and no way to avoid getting lost. Considering my options, I realized that if events were going to repeat themselves, I only had a few minutes before the creepy hooded lady came out of the lake. Coming up with a plan, I ducked just behind the tree line to make me harder to spot. Keeping an eye on the center of the lake, I worked my way around it, hidden from sight in the trees. I took great care to be quiet, pausing every time I stepped over a twig. And I tried my best to ignore the occasional noises coming from the darkness behind me.

I stopped when I was about a quarter of the way around the lake and crouched behind a bush. Settling in, I made sure I was ready to make a mad dash out of here, if it came to that.

I didn't have to wait long. After a few minutes, the middle of the lake started bubbling, sending ripples toward the shoreline, just like before. The froth turned into a geyser erupting from the lake, and when the fountain stopped, the woman stood there. Same as before, a hood covered her face, and she was carrying a small body in her arms. She shook off the water and stalked toward the far shore.

I still couldn't see her face, but her posture was ramrod straight, reminding me of a former classmate who did ballet. This woman's movement was full of that same liquid dancer's grace. But underneath the grace, there was a hint of predatory nature. I found myself thinking of a tiger I'd seen in a zoo once, restlessly pacing behind a thick plexiglass wall. When our eyes met, I knew it'd crush my skull in its jaws given half the chance. This woman moved with the same sense of ruthless purpose.

I shivered despite myself. Taking a deep breath to calm my nerves, I weighed my options. My instincts warned me to be cautious, fighting a fierce battle with my need to get a better view. After a few moments, curiosity won out. I inched around the lake, still in the shadows behind the tree line. Whether my fear was irrational or not, I didn't want to alert her to my presence.

Once I was closer, I stopped to take another look. The veiled woman was almost to the shoreline now—twenty or thirty feet away. At this angle, it was clear that the bundle she was holding was indeed a person. My eyes widened and I bit back a gasp of horror. It was a child who couldn't be any more than ten, with fine blond hair hanging from his lolling head. Studying him closer, I could see a hint of movement, telling me he was still breathing. I also noticed he was wearing modern clothing, in sharp contrast with the woman's old-school hooded cloak.

Once she reached the shoreline, she set the boy down and gave her sleeves a brisk shake, revealing hands that glowed ghostly under the moonlight. Her long, slender fingers made me think of spiders, and I shivered again as she pulled back her hood. Unfortunately, she'd turned away from me when she set the boy down. I couldn't see her face, no matter how I angled myself. All I could see was a head of sleek, pin-straight, silvery-blonde hair.

Fear clashed again with my need to know more. After a moment's hesitation, I crept a little closer, hoping to at least see her profile. High, prominent cheekbones came into view, but I couldn't see anything more. Frustrated, I edged forward a few more feet. In my clumsiness, a twig snapped, the noise reverberating across the glassy surface of the lake. I froze, swearing at myself in my head. The woman's head shot up and she scanned the shoreline in front of her, looking for the source of the noise. Her head swiveled, turning toward me. Back at my hiding spot, I was panicking—she was going to sense my presence, she'd know I was watching, and that would be that.

I sat up in bed, gasping. Early morning light hit my eyes, the type a night owl like me almost never saw. It might have been far too early for my taste, but at least it was light out, which meant I didn't feel obligated to go back to sleep and revisit that lake.

Going over the dream in my head, I stood up and stretched. Maybe I *should* have bought that book. Then again, if I'd done that, I'd have to explain to Logan why I was reading it. I didn't think he would have bought "I want to get in touch with my roots" as an explanation. He knew me better than that. Given the havoc they'd wrought on my life, I was quite content to just use my talents for practical purposes without knowing anything more about where they came from.

Feeling twitchy, I decided to get out for a while. Rifling through the laundry pile, I found a cleanish smelling shirt and pulled on the jeans I'd bought the day before. Add fingerless gloves and boots, and I was ready to go. Before I left, I threw on my favorite hoodie to ward off the morning chill. Solid black, lots of zippered pockets, and a hood so deep it swallowed my face. It was great for going incognito, especially when combined with the pair of sunglasses I'd fished out from the pile when I grabbed the shirt. The fewer facial features people could see, the easier it was to keep up a glamour.

Sticking my head out into the hallway, I saw Logan's door was still shut, which meant he was asleep. Good. He wouldn't notice my leaving at this ungodly hour and have any awkward questions.

Down the stairs, no twitchy kids in the stairwell this time, out the door, and onto the streets. Our quarantine was a ghost town at this time of day. None of us had "real" jobs to go to. But to allow for the existence of gainful employment (even though nobody would hire us), the curfew was lifted at 6:00 a.m. on weekdays. That meant I was free to go as I pleased.

I retraced our path from the previous day and headed to the bookstore. Dismayed, I found out it didn't open for another hour and a half. I hadn't even thought of that possibility, since I was never up this early. Glancing around the street, I spotted a small combination cafe and convenience store across from the bookstore. That'd be as good a place to kill time as any.

I bought the smallest, cheapest coffee they sold, determined to nurse it as long as possible. I parked myself at one of the outside tables and took a tiny sip, keeping an eye on the bookstore. I wanted to head over right when it opened; I was hoping to get back before Logan woke up and started wondering where I was.

Given that I'd covered most of my features, it took almost no energy to do a simple "nothing to see" glamour. If a bystander looked at me, their eyes would slide right off. They'd remember seeing someone, but their memory would stop there. Even if they'd interacted with me, as the sweet cashier had. She'd remember me as one blurry face in a day full of customers, and nothing more.

The "nothing to see" glamour stopped just shy of full-blown invisibility. Invisibility sounded cool, but as every young Marked found out, it never worked well in practice. It took a lot of energy, for one. For another, people would walk into you or try to sit on you. That gets old fast. And if you lost concentration for any reason, you'd have a hard time explaining yourself to bystanders who'd seen the patch of sidewalk suddenly sprout a person.

While I waited, I people-watched. I was surprised at how bustling the neighborhood was this early in the morning. Maybe it wasn't that shocking, and I was just out of the loop. It'd been a long time since I'd been around normal people on a weekday morning, after all. Kids walked with their parents, keeping up an incessant stream of chatter as they were herded to the bus stop. An elderly lady walked a tiny dog that looked for all the world like a stuffed animal. The ear-piercing yips proved it wasn't one.

As I watched these people, a little jealous of their mundane lives, one woman caught my eye. Her eyes were puffy and red-rimmed, and she was carrying a small stack of paper, walking with purpose. She looked young, maybe five or six years older than me, mid to late twenties. I ducked back in after her when she walked into the café, my interest piqued. Sipping my way-too-bitter coffee, I stood at the end of the counter in a low-traffic spot where nobody would notice me and watched her.

As she waited in line, she picked at a stray thread at the bottom of her shirt. We weren't in a nice neighborhood, but her clothes looked a little more worn than most. Worn, but spotless. I recognized the look—poor but proud. And then she was at the counter, talking with the cashier.

"Hi. I'm wondering if you have a community bulletin board?"

The cashier snapped her gum. "Yeah, over there. But I have to get the manager to approve any postings, and she's not in until noon. Why, what've you got?"

The woman's lip quivered, but she bit it and soldiered on, maintaining her composure. "My son . . . is missing. Since last night. We went to bed, and when I woke up, he just wasn't there. I've reported it to the police, but they aren't taking it too seriously. His dad . . ." She sniffed, then stopped herself and pressed her mouth into a thin line. "But I can tell that's not what happened this time. I'd like to put up a few posters, in case anyone has seen him. He's a good kid, but sometimes he likes to wander." Her voice was hopeful with a neurotic, frayed edge.

The cashier had clearly been expecting a poster about some kind of class or job fair. Her detachment turned into sympathy and concern. "Of course. It's no problem. Let me put that up for you right now."

She took the poster from the distraught mother and reached out with her other hand to squeeze her arm. It was clear this act of kindness from a stranger almost did her in.

Fighting to keep her emotions under control, she blinked a few times, tilted her chin up, and said, "Thank you, I appreciate it. When I find him, I'll call you so you can take the poster down."

The cashier nodded and watched her leave. She took the next customer's order, then walked over to the bulletin board and put the poster up, shaking her head. As she returned to the counter, I tossed my empty coffee cup in the trash. Despite my best efforts to make it last, I'd already drained it of all caffeinated sustenance. I didn't know what made me look, because I knew it was going to depress me, but I walked over to the bulletin board. It sounded like a deadbeat dad "borrowing" a kid in a power play to get back at mom for coming out better in a custody battle. Not likely to get a lot of police attention, especially since he was from the bad part of town.

The cashier, bless her heart, had put the poster front and center, crowding out the flyers for yoga classes and sliding-scale therapists. The headline read, "Missing Child: Andrew Jones," followed by the woman's contact information and when Andrew was last seen. I glanced at the photo, and my stomach dropped to somewhere below my feet. I staggered backward, almost tripping on a chair.

The kid on the poster was the same child I'd seen in my dream last night. I recognized the same blond hair, the same chubby face. I think he was even wearing the same damn hoodie.

In my shock, I must have dropped my glamour. An old lady who shouldn't have noticed me or my reaction reached out to pat my arm.

"Distressing, isn't it? It's always sad when a child goes missing. I know Charlene, she's such a nice woman. She does the best she can with what she has. Raising that child, she had him so young, and his father . . . " She shook her head, clucking her tongue in disapproval. "He's a piece of work. But Charlene is a good woman and she loves that boy. She'll get him back, don't you worry." She patted my arm again and gave me a reassuring smile, showing rows of yellowed dentures.

I swallowed hard, made a noise of agreement, and nodded. Taking a deep breath, I forced myself back into the glamour, and the woman's eyes slipped right over me as she glanced around the café. I made a beeline for the door, not caring who I bumped into and hearing a few annoyed grumbles as a result. Under normal circumstances, I wouldn't be so hasty, but they'd just blame it on whoever was standing closest to them. Or on their lack of caffeine.

Back outside, I leaned against the side of the building, forcing myself to slow down my breathing and hating the panicked tightness in my chest. Looking up, I saw the bookstore was now open. I felt stuck between my conflicting desires to learn more and to go hide at home and breathe into a paper bag. This *couldn't* be a coincidence.

I pushed myself away from the wall and pulled my chin up high, mimicking the composure of that woman, Charlene. If she could be that calm with a missing kid, I could be calm enough to dig around in a bookstore to get some answers. I strode across the street and into the store. The same owlish man from the day before saw me, but didn't *see* me as I marched toward the Folklore and Mythology section. He gave a brief grunt that I translated as, "I'm acknowledging your presence as a potential customer, but I'm also going to go back to my reading now."

I searched the shelves and yanked the encyclopedia from its perch, along with a few other volumes that looked promising. Dragging out a stepstool, I settled down and dug into the book.

An hour later, I had nothing useful and was fighting the

urge to throw a full-on temper tantrum in the aisle. The "Lake, Lady of" entry consisted only of references to the Arthurian legends. I should have guessed that, but I'd thought maybe there'd be notes on the origins of the legend. Wells and springs were often shown as doorways to the underworld (or other-world). Water was often linked with goddesses and feminine magic. Blah, blah, blah—all useless, most of it irrelevant. Even the bits about portals to the otherworld, though interesting and potentially applicable, didn't give me any ideas for action.

I'd even looked into myths and stories involving child abduction. There were several entries, but they were all about one kidnapping at a time, a la changelings. I had dreamed of another kid, before Andrew . . . Had that child gone missing, too? The Pied Piper was the only reference I could find to group enchantments, and the creepy hooded lady didn't seem like the musical sort.

I gave up. Sticking the books back on the shelves in the same order I'd pulled them off, I threw my hood back up and put my sunglasses back on. Leaving the store, I dou-ble-checked to make sure I hadn't accidentally dropped the glamour in my irritation. The last thing I needed was anyone stopping me on my way back.

I wandered down the street and headed toward home, so lost in my thoughts I almost tripped over the railroad tracks. By the time I got back to the apartment, it was only an hour or so later than when I normally woke up. As luck would have it, Logan was sitting at the kitchen table, flipping through an old, beat-up magazine. He spared a look at me as I walked in the front door.

"Keeping up with current events?" I said, leaning on the table. Sometimes, only having one chair for your kitchen table is a problem.

"You know me, always on top of the times," he replied

with a wry smile. I found this particularly entertaining coming from someone who had never seen a television or witnessed the wonders of internal plumbing before we met.

"So," he continued, slapping the magazine shut and leaning back in his chair, "where'd you get off to at such an early hour? I'm pretty sure I heard you leaving just after sunrise. Since when are you an early bird?"

"I . . . had another bad dream," I said, scrunching up my face. Damn those unnatural elf ears.

His face softened. "Another one about your mom?"

I sighed. "No, not about her. I've been having these upsetting dreams. I'm not sure they're just dreams anymore, but they're not like my typical . . . prophetic dreams." I almost choked on the word "prophetic," which seemed pretentious and unnatural, but was the closest word I could think of. Logan quirked an eyebrow, indicating for me to continue. I didn't want to elaborate, but he might have some ideas. And for my part, I was starting to feel a little desperate after my fruitless research session earlier.

I told him about the dream, pausing several times, and waited for him to laugh at how silly I sounded. He was still looking at me with no sign of mirth, so I continued. "I thought I'd go back into town and do more research, and there was a missing child poster at the café. The kid . . . Logan, it was the same one I saw in my dream."

I looked up, not sure what facial expression I'd see, praying for anything but horror. After having been reminded of my mother's reaction to that first awful dream, I wouldn't be able to cope with Logan looking at me like that. The look I saw on my wisecracking roommate's face wasn't one I'd seen very often—maybe never. His eyes were wide and concerned, and he was biting his lip. I decided horror might have been a little less unsettling, after all.

"Are you sure you didn't. . . I don't know . . . fill in the blanks?" he asked, as though he was puzzling it out as he spoke. "Like, the kid in your dream just looked like a typical kid. Then, when you saw the poster today, you were so worked up that you decided he looked like the same kid?"

"No way," I said with an emphatic shake of my head. "I'm positive. It was the same kid. I remember his hair, his face. He was even wearing the same hoodie. I'm sure."

He leaned forward. "Tania, I need you to tell me everything about the woman in your dream."

I sighed. "I didn't see much of her face at all. She has straight hair. It's kind of a silvery blonde. If she were a normal person, I'd say she's paying someone a hell of a lot of money to make her hair look like that." I paused, struggling to drum up more details from my memory. "She's pale. She has high cheekbones that stuck out." I sucked in my cheeks to demonstrate. "Past that . . . " I shrugged, frustrated. "In both dreams, she wore this ridiculous cloak that hid her body. She's about this tall?" I raised my arm above my head but just below Logan's. "That's about all I've got."

He leaned back in the chair again and crossed his arms, his lips pursed. "I bet it's nothing. You should just ignore it."

I scoffed. "Seriously, Logan? You were just asking questions like it was a *very* big deal. You *know* I've got a proven track record with dreams—"

He interrupted, dismissing my response with a wave of his hand. "Whatever. If you want to get all worked up about it when it's probably just a weird coincidence, that's your call. But it doesn't sound like anything to me."

I stared at him, baffled at his complete turnaround, my mouth hanging open. "Excuse me? And what if another kid goes missing?"

His eyes flashed brilliant green in irritation. "It's not your problem. And like I said, I don't think it's anything. Now, if you'll excuse me, I have places to be and things to do." As he spoke, he somehow managed to stand up, grab the magazine, and exit the room in one smooth motion. The door closed behind him precisely as he finished, cutting off any room for further argument. Elfin grace was a hell of a way to get the last word in. Not fair.

I was left staring at the door, furious at my best friend's hostility. And after he'd asked me to describe the woman and everything. I slumped to the floor and pulled my knees up, burying my face in them. There was something weird going on here, I was sure of that. Given that assumption, what were my options? I could try to see if another kid had disappeared— the first one I'd dreamed about. The problem was, I didn't see any good way to do that without knowing what he looked like. Especially not without coming off like a total psycho, which was a dangerous thing for a Marked. Reaching out to Andrew's mom sounded like a recipe for disaster, too.

Lifting my head, I realized two things. Number one, we needed to clean more often. The state of this floor was a little horrifying. Number two, if I wanted to prevent this from happening again, my only option was to talk to the authorities. Or try to, anyway. There was no guarantee they'd listen to me, or help. Or even be *able* to help. But it was looking like the best option thus far.

I stood up, groaning. It wasn't even noon and I was leaving my house for the second time that day. This is what happens when you wake up early. Heaving a dramatic sigh received only by an empty room, I walked out the door, hoping this wasn't going to be as fruitless as I expected it to be.

# CHAPTER FIVE

hated cops. And I was pretty sure they hated me. Looking like a suspicious ragamuffin didn't exactly inspire confidence with the boys in blue. Add being Marked on top of that and . . . well.

The security guards around our quarantine were like cops, but worse. Take the standard "us vs. them" attitude and turn it up to eleven. They were high on self-righteousness and delusions of grandeur. If you asked them, they were preventing the downfall of society by keeping us freaks locked in at night, caged and leashed.

Given that, I was not looking forward to this conversation. Walking to the guards' offices, my stomach felt like it housed a lead weight the size of Montana. I'd never been there before—why would I *want* to?—but we all knew where it was. It was hard to miss, given that it was the only building inside our quarantine that wasn't falling apart.

I reached the gate kiosk and pressed the buzzer. The

gate seemed to be designed for cars, not pedestrian traffic. I imagined they didn't get a lot of neighbors dropping by with brownies.

A skinny guy with greasy skin and even greasier brown hair appeared at the window and gave me a skeptical once-over. The building was small but raised off the ground, forcing him to literally look down at me.

The intercom crackled. "Yes?"

"Uh. Hi." I wiped my sweaty palms on my jeans, hoping he didn't notice. Looking nervous wasn't going to make him less suspicious. "Can I talk to someone in charge?"

He sneered at me, doubt mixing with exasperation on his face. "If you have any concerns, I assure you that I am fully qualified to note them down. Are you here about the lack of a dumpster by building 5A? We've already submitted the paper-work for that request. It will be processed through the proper channels in due time."

I resisted the urge to roll my eyes. Paperwork? Please. Instead, I took a measured breath, trying to maintain my composure, and pressed on.

"I have information about a kidnapping. A child that's gone missing. I thought I should come to you," I replied, try-ing to force both confidence and urgency into my voice.

His look was still skeptical, but a little less so. Crossing his arms, he stared at me through the thick plexiglass, waiting for me to either recant or elaborate. I refused to do either. If I was going to go through all this trouble, I was going to tell what I knew to someone who could do something about it, not a ki-osk-dwelling pencil pusher. Holding my chin high to meet his eyes, I looked right back at him, unblinking.

I was better than most at winning staring contests, and he gave in before I did. He pursed his lips while looking me over again, indecision flickering on his face, and then disappeared from view. A second later, a buzzer sounded and the gate opened. Taking a few careful steps forward, I saw Mr. Kiosk standing at the entrance to his little station, waving me over.

He was speaking into a walkie-talkie on his shoulder. "We've got an 092 here at the gate. Says she has information on a kidnapping. Can I get a level three official out here?"

And then we waited, in thick, uncomfortable silence. I rocked on my feet, trying not to fidget any more than that. After five minutes that inched by slower than cold molasses, two men in uniform approached us. The one on the right was tall and muscular, but in a lean-runner sort of way. He had a shock of ginger-blond hair sticking out at every angle and a sprinkle of light freckles across a narrow nose. The other guy was shorter and built like a buff boulder, dark-haired and in-tense. They were both walking in a slow, purposeful manner, examining me with a mix of interest and disdain. The lead pit in my belly grew heavier.

"Is this the 092?" Boulder asked Kiosk. *Rude.* I was right there.

"Yep," replied Kiosk. Boulder cocked his head and raised his eyebrows. Kiosk hurried to amend himself, adding, "Uh, yes, *sir.*"

Boulder glanced at me, then back to Kiosk. "Mind if we use your office? The prelim questioning won't take long."

Kiosk nodded nervously, sidestepping out of the way to let us by.

I followed the two officers in and was surprised at how cramped it was on the inside. Freckles sat in the swiveling office chair, leaving Boulder to stand at his side and glower at me. I had to stand, leaning against the desk while trying not to fidget.

Boulder was the first to speak. "ID?"

I took my ID out of my pocket and handed it to Freckles.

He scanned it, grunted, and handed it to Boulder. As Boulder looked it over, Freckles leaned back in his chair and said, "I'm Officer Tennant." He jerked his chin at Boulder. "This is Officer Minear. What did you come here to tell us?"

I tried to swallow, but my mouth was dry. "It sounds kinda crazy, but I've been having these dreams about missing children. And then today in town I saw a poster of the same kid that I dreamed about last night. And I just thought you all should know, because it doesn't seem like a normal case . . ." I trailed off as I looked from one officer's face to the other. Neither looked impressed. In fact, Tennant was scowling at me as if I'd been rolling in garbage and had tracked it in here. I swallowed again and forced myself to finish the thought. "The kid's name is Andrew. Don't you want to look it up?"

The two men glanced at each other. After a beat, Boulder—er, Minear—nodded. "I'll go check on that."

He left the kiosk, presumably to go make a call. Now that he was gone, I wasn't sure if I felt more or less comfortable. Before, I didn't like the two-against-one odds. Now, I *really* didn't like the way Tennant was looking at me, openly disgusted. Talk about awkward silence.

He spoke first. "You know you're probably just wasting our time, right? Coming in here with stupid stories and expecting us to look into them? The only reason we didn't kick you out immediately was because a child could be involved."

I tried to keep my face straight and my voice calm as I replied. "I know it could be nothing." I paused, then added "sir" as an afterthought, trying hard not to sound sarcastic. "But I'm telling you, it was the same kid." Against my better judgment, I pressed on, desperate for him to see my side of things. I just wanted to focus on the boy, who was probably lost and scared and needed our help. "If it were a normal dream or I were a normal person, that'd be one thing, but my dreams—"

Without warning, Tennant stood up and leaned into my face, his chair skittering away behind him. In my rush to back away, I almost ran into a filing cabinet, my arms out in the universal symbol for "Don't shoot!"

"If you were a *normal* person," Tennant growled, "I wouldn't even be here. I'd have a *normal* cop job. I wouldn't be stuck at this office, dealing with you freaks day in and day out. Wondering when one of you is going to snap and pull some satanic bullshit on me or my buddies."

This was not going well. I looked over Tennant's shoulder at the exit, hoping Minear would walk in and put a stop to this before it got worse. I glanced back to see Tennant stalking around the desk toward me.

"If you ask me"—he was already too close for comfort and punctuated each word with a step in my direction—"we should just round you all up and put you on an island."

I was starting to weigh escape routes, feeling the flush of adrenaline slowing time down. I opened my mouth to reply, "If it makes you feel any better, I'd be fine with that." But before I could speak, he added, "And then bomb the hell out of it." At this point, his nose was millimeters from mine, and my back was pressed against the cold metal of the filing cabinet.

"Uh, look," I stammered, "I was just trying to help, okay?"

He cut me off with a sucker punch to the stomach. *This* was why I didn't like cops. I doubled over, wheezing, and ran through my options at lightning speed. Couldn't glamour him, how would I get away and past the other guy? Maybe I could scream and hope one of the other guards would take pity? I straightened up, still clutching my stomach, and took a painful breath in to yell for help, but Tennant saw that coming. He cut me off with a hand around my throat, lifting me off my feet and pushing me back into the corner I'd trapped myself in.

"You *people*. You make me sick. You know what? You don't

even deserve to be called people." A slow grin spread across his face. "If you were a real person, this wouldn't hurt you the way it does."

As I tore at his hands, a bright glint of silver caught my eye. In his free hand, Tennant was holding a nasty-looking knife, tinged with black along its razor-sharp blade. Oh no. This was about to get a *lot* worse.

He laughed when he saw the fear on my face. "You know what this is, don't you?"

Indeed, I did. I'd seen savvy street merchants hawking them after some enterprising soul discovered all Marked were sensitive to iron. It was a knife made out of pure iron—far more painful than any horseshoe.

Tennant was more unhinged than I'd given him credit for. This called for drastic measures. A glamour wasn't going to get me out of my current situation, held up against a wall with my vision tunneling from lack of oxygen. I screwed up my face and concentrated all my adrenaline-fueled survival instincts into shifting. Just one spot: my left hand, which I angled away from him. Focusing on my face, he lifted the knife closer. Sinews stretched and twisted, bones cracked and reformed, and my left hand morphed into a claw, one that looked like it belonged to a gargoyle. Thick, scaly skin, resistant to knives, and, most useful here, jagged nails at the tip of each finger. This particular form had worked well for me before, and I was hoping it'd save my bacon again.

Tennant pressed the flat of the blade into my right cheek. If I'd had the air to spare, I would have screamed. Purified iron was the worst. I could feel my skin heating with a painful chemical-burn feeling. I tried to wrench my face away, but he had me pinned within his grasp. He was laughing again—but not for long. I drew my hand back, preparing to swipe at his face and hopefully take the asshole's nose off, when the door opened.

"Tennant!" roared his partner.

Tennant dropped me in a heap on the floor and spun around, panting. I rolled away from them, trying to get away, but didn't have a whole lot of room, given that he'd backed me into a corner. Instead, I took several gasping breaths and hid my harpy hand, focusing on changing it back before they saw it.

"She came at me!" Tennant shouted. Of *course* I did. If I'd had the energy to spare, I'd have rolled my eyes at that old chestnut: crazed, violent Marked on the loose!

Minear surveyed the scene, his eyes darting from Tennant to me, the handprint around my neck, and the red welt on my face. I glowered at both of them, my throat still too raw to speak.

"The missing child has been ruled a likely parental kidnapping," Minear said to me, "and the appropriate amount of resources have been allocated to find him." Done with me, he turned to Tennant. "Do you have any idea how much paperwork we'd have to file if you'd seriously injured her?"

They glared at each other, mano a mano. Over in my corner, I coughed, testing my throat.

"Now that I've had the crap beat out of me for trying to be a responsible citizen, can I go?" I rasped. Maybe sarcasm wasn't the best course of action right now. But at this point, I was ready to glamour them both stupid and walk out, and do the same to anyone who got in my way between here and home.

"You're not a *full* citizen," sneered Tennant.

I'd recovered enough to reply with an emphatic eye roll.

Minear stepped between us and gestured to the door. "Yes. You can let yourself out now, thank you." He turned back to Tennant. If only looks could kill. I got the impression that someone was going to get a brisk talking-to when I left, even if it was just about the damn paperwork.

I staggered toward the door, in no small hurry to get out of there. On my way out, I ran into the former occupant of the kiosk, hovering around and trying to look like he hadn't been listening in. When he saw me, Kiosk started to look away, embarrassed at being caught in the act of eavesdropping. As I walked by, he snuck a glance at me and forgot his embarrassment, staring at my injuries with his mouth hanging open. I responded by giving him the finger and pulling up my hood to cover the angry red marks on my face and neck.

Fifteen long, painful minutes later, I was back home, wishing we had some frozen veggies to use as an ice pack. Instead, I ended up wrapping some ice cubes in a dirty washcloth and holding it against my face. Apparently, *this* is what happens when you try to do the right thing. I stared out the window, trying to figure out what I could do from here, or if I should just give up. Seemed like a solid dead end at this point until I had more to go on.

The door opened behind me, but I ignored it. Logan didn't greet me, either; he must have been still trying to give me the cold shoulder. The size of our kitchen made that a little difficult, and in his close squeeze by the kitchen table, he got a full view of my battle wounds. I looked up when I heard the soft thud of a Western novel hitting the floor and was met with Logan's concerned face, peering at me from inches away.

"Dude, what are you *doing*?" I snapped. "Don't you people believe in personal space?" My sore throat forced me to whisper, but I'd be damned if an injury would take away my snarkiness.

"What *happened*, Tania?" His eyes dropped down to the bruising around my neck. "Who did this to you? I swear. I'll . . . I'll flay them. How did they get away with this?"

I sighed, which made me cough again. "I was alone with one of the guards, who turned out to be crazier than a bag of rats." I paused to give my throat a rest. "He decided to take out his frustrations with all of Marked-kind on me, I guess."

"Oh, Tania. I'm so sorry. This is my fault."

"Yeah, I kinda knew that already," I snarled back. Logan and I didn't fight often, but I was pretty peeved at him at that particular moment.

"Here . . . " Logan removed the wet rag from my face and brushed his fingers against the shiny red welt. Still scowling, I leaned back to let him take a better look. "Ouch. He used iron?" I nodded, wincing from his touch. "Well, that will have to heal on its own. I can help with this, though."

He placed a hand on my neck and closed his eyes. I looked out the window again, trying not to flash back to that other set of hands around my throat. A cooling sensation trickled its way across my neck, sinking into the skin and soothing my throat. Logan stood back and admired his handiwork with a self-satisfied smile. "There! See? Don't say I never did anything for you."

I made a few short "ahems" to test my healed throat. When I found everything was back in working order, I decided to celebrate my returned-to-normal voice by yelling at the top of my lungs. "Oh *really*? I wouldn't have even gone to the guards if you hadn't acted like I was a crazy person! All you had to do was listen to me, but noooo . . . "

He wrinkled his nose. "Grudges don't suit you, Tania. I mean, I wish I hadn't reacted like that. But didn't I just make it up to you?"

This was probably as close to an apology as I was going to get, so I figured I'd take it. I heaved a dramatic sigh to demonstrate exactly how much effort it was taking to be so forgiving. Crossing my arms, I said, "Okay, fine. Why did you act like that, anyway? You seemed interested and then—"

This time, I cut myself off before letting him do it. I hadn't even finished my sentence and his body language had already shifted from "self-satisfied with a hint of apology" to "closed off tighter than Fort Knox." Even though I was baffled by his touchiness, I was too tired to argue with him again after the day I'd had. I switched subjects. "Anything interesting going on tonight?"

Definitely not the smoothest segue ever, but Logan was willing to roll with it. Brightening up, he told me about the poker game tonight where he was going to rake in the cash. He even invited me to the game, but I declined. Poker wasn't my thing.

I did decide to work that night, though, and most of the nights that week. The average weeknight was slow—people trolling bars at midnight on a Tuesday didn't often have enough money in their wallets to make it worth the work. But my hope was that maybe if I worked all night, every night, I'd be too exhausted to have any more creepy dreams.

So I put on my game-face glamour each night, especially important now that I was sporting an ugly welt. Several of the nights were slow, but I stayed out, anyway, sometimes switching tactics—gambling on pool instead of picking pockets. Some nights, I cleaned up against all odds. Wednesday was especially notable, when I encountered a despicable cab driver with a fat wad of cash (and a small baggie of drugs) in his wallet. I kept the cash and flushed the drugs. The last thing I needed on my conscience was for Jake to find them in the trash and OD.

By Friday, my overactive work schedule had taken its toll, grinding me into the ground. All week, I'd been getting in around five in the morning, and then I couldn't seem to sleep past ten or eleven. In fact, I was surprised the iron burn had almost healed, given the combination of overwork and lack of sleep. On the bright side, I had more money than usual and hadn't had any more freaky dreams. That was good enough for me.

In between the exhaustion and the extra cash, I decided to stay in, even though it was usually a high-earning night. Logan tried to get me to go out with him, but I refused. He'd been doing well with his poker games and wanted to treat me to a night on the town, probably motivated by his lingering guilt. I appreciated it, though. Any other night I would have taken him up on it, but I couldn't drag myself out of the house. After several valiant efforts to woo me, he gave up and teased me on his way out about how much I'd miss.

Come eight o'clock, I was sitting in bed, sipping hot cocoa and surrounded by worn magazines that I'd already read. Warm, fuzzy sleep embraced me, and I welcomed it with open arms. My paranoia had finally worn off, and I was *so* tired.

At first, my dreams were a jumble of memories: the first night I slept on cold concrete, the day I met Logan. The smirk on his face as he said, "That glamour may have worked on *that* imbecile, but it won't work on anyone else. Your technique is atrocious." The first time we'd had any extra money. We bought ice cream and ate it until we were almost sick, reveling in the luxury of buying something that wasn't a necessity. Lying on the floor, I said that my stomach might actually explode if I had another bite (as I reached for the carton). I blinked, laughing through the nausea, and then everything went sideways.

When reality righted itself, I was on my knees in the same godforsaken forest, crouching behind a bush. Something was different this time, though—I wasn't half-weightless as I had been before. I was *here*. Snow soaked through my pants and stung my palms, and my ears tingled with the cold. I stood up, wiping my hands on my jeans. I looked around and wondered what had brought me back here. Maybe this was just an especially vivid dream? A second ago, I'd been full of ice cream and *that* had felt authentic enough.

Since I was here, I might as well see if I could learn anything new. If I didn't get frostbite first, anyway. I examined my surroundings. In the first two dreams, I'd landed right by the lake. This time, I was back in the woods a bit, the shimmering surface of the lake peeking through the trees on my left. I slogged through the snow toward the water, gaining a sudden appreciation of how much time I'd saved before. The snowfall might have only been calf-high, but I was getting a workout trudging through it.

With effort, I made it to the edge of the trees around the lake. Stopping just behind the tree line to stay hidden, I worked my way around the lake, hoping that I was in the same spot as before. I positioned myself so that, if I remembered everything correctly, I'd be right in front of the woman when she appeared. Assuming I could manage to stay quiet (and stop my teeth from chattering) long enough, I'd be able to get a good look at her face. Maybe then I could get some answers.

I settled in behind a tree and waited a few minutes, my legs tingling from the cold, but the lake was still smooth as glass. I didn't know if I was early or if she was late. Or maybe this *was* just a dream. At any rate, having a minute to catch my breath reminded me to put up a protective glamour. I closed my eyes and took a moment to reach for my internal wellspring of energy. In a twist I wasn't expecting, it was far easier than normal—I hardly had to concentrate. It was so easy, I was a little concerned it hadn't taken. I didn't have any time to test it, though, because now the lake was rippling and frothing in the telltale signs that Her Hooded Creepiness was about to join us.

My guesstimate was spot-on. I had a full view of the woman's face, who was again carrying what I now easily recognized as an unconscious child. She glided toward my hiding spot, leaving no ripples behind her watery footsteps. Reaching the shore, she set the child down. I didn't look at the little body— I was focused on her face, hoping to see something I hadn't been able to before.

She rolled her head and stretched her shoulders, lifting her hood as she did so. It fell back onto her shoulders, giving me my first good look at her features. There were the high, haughty cheekbones and silvery-blonde hair. I could also see a sharp chin and a delicate, straight nose. Her eyes looked like they'd been cut from the heart of a glacier—blue-white irises rimmed in black. Overall, she was beautiful, but in the way a marble sculpture was beautiful. Aesthetically pleasing, but not something you'd want to hug. Her expression was cold, detached, and entirely inhuman.

I shuddered despite myself. My eyes dropped to the child, trying to note any distinct features that I could use to investigate when I got back home. *If* I made it back home. This snow (and my soaked jeans) were definitely and inconveniently real. As I peered at the tiny body, the woman shifted, letting the full moon's light shine on the child's face. I nearly fell backward with shock, grabbing the tree I was hiding behind to keep me upright. I knew that face—the golden-brown skin, dark lashes, thick, straight hair, and round little cheeks.

It was Alejandro. My buddy from the market. Rosa's nephew.

Panicking, I tried to scramble back, adrenaline pumping through my veins, making me shake—and found myself sitting up in bed, panting hard, early morning sunlight bright in my eyes.

# CHAPTER SIX

The pants I'd fallen asleep in were still soaked up to the knees, erasing any lingering doubts (or hopes) that it *was* just a dream.

"Logan!" I bellowed at the top of my lungs. I stampeded across the hallway and swung open his bedroom door. A quick glance at the unused sheets on his bed told me all I needed to know—he was probably still at that damn poker game. When he got back, he'd know what to do, I was sure of it. Logan was cool-headed in any situation, always with a smart solution at hand.

But, in the meantime, I was determined to get some answers. Maybe it wasn't Alejandro. Maybe it *was* just a dream. I mean, I wasn't a bed-wetter, so I had no idea how my pants had gotten soaked from ankle to knee, but maybe there was a reason and I was missing it. I'd been working hard and was stressed out all week. I was on my last frayed nerve—maybe that had something to do with it. I barked out a hoarse laugh as my theory-spitting mind suggested maybe I'd manifested a new ability out of stress. Conjuring water in my sleep, *that* would come in handy for sure.

My theories only got more outlandish from there. I tried to reassure myself, dashing around the apartment and changing into clothes semisuitable for public. I caught a glance at myself as I ran past the lone mirror in our apartment. My reflection looked unkempt and bordering on crazy. Dark circles shadowed my red eyes, my outfit was mismatched and rumpled, and my sleep-ruffled hair completed the ensemble. Whatever, I didn't have time to fix this mess. I grabbed my hoodie and zipped it up, throwing the hood up in an attempt to at least cover the bedhead.

I went over the events again as I ran-walked to the market. Judging by the sun peeking over the tops of the buildings, I should make it there right after they opened. With any luck, there wouldn't be many people around, and I could talk to Rosa alone for a few minutes.

Ten minutes (that felt like hours) later, I was at the entrance, showing my ID to the guard and standing on tiptoe to look over his shoulder and see if I could spot Rosa. He waved me through, even as he gave me a weird look—he probably didn't get many customers that eager to snag some good produce. I stopped just short of running around like a maniac, but power-walked up and down the aisles, glancing at each stand as I went by. Not Rosa, not Rosa, not Rosa . . . Was she not here?

Finally, I spotted her—she was in a different aisle than normal, with her back to me.

"Rosa!" I yelled as I ran toward her stand. She turned around, confused.

"Oh, hello, dear." She surveyed my state of distress with concern in her eyes. "What's the matter? Are you okay?"

"Hi Rosa," I panted. "Look, I know this is going to sound crazy, but where's Alejandro? Is he okay? Is he missing?"

Her puzzled look told me she had no idea what I was talking about. "Sweetie, as far as I know, Alejandro is fine. Why? What happened? Here, you need some water."

She rifled through a duffle bag and pulled out a bottle of water, twisting off the cap as she handed it to me. I took it gratefully, nodding in thanks, and drained half the bottle in one gulp.

"I'm sorry, Rosa," I said, once I'd caught my breath. "I've been . . . like I said, I know it sounds crazy. But I've been having these awful dreams, and I thought maybe something had happened to him. I didn't mean to freak you out. I just wanted to make sure that he was okay. Are you sure he's safe? You should tell your sister to keep an eye on him, just in case."

"Alejandro is *fine*, Tania." Rosa moved around behind me and patted my shoulder. "Now, I can tell even without asking that you haven't been sleeping well. You look sick—you need some rest. I want you to—" Rosa was interrupted by her phone dinging with a text. She glanced at the table behind us. "Just a second, let me get that."

Relieved, I wondered if maybe it *was* just a dream. The hyperreality and real-world aftereffects could be new Marked side effects I hadn't figured out yet. Or maybe it was a warning. If so, at least we could do something about it. I glanced at Rosa, who was studying her phone with her eyebrows knit together, chewing her lip.

"Uh, is everything okay?" I asked.

She waved my concern away, but the worried look lingered on her face. "Yes. I think so. My sister just asked me to call her. Let me see if I can get a good signal. You can shop around, you don't have to wait for me."

Hanging back at the booth as she walked away, I was

torn between wanting to give Rosa privacy and wanting to eavesdrop on the call. I'd started to calm down after her reassurances, but now my worries were starting to tap-dance around in my head again. Fixing my eyes on a pile of potatoes, I stared at it like it'd tell me what was going on if I just glared hard enough.

The minutes crept by. What seemed like an eternity later, I heard Rosa walking back over to the stall. Afraid to look, I forced myself to stop gazing at the potatoes and focus on her face. It was obvious that something was wrong. She looked dazed, and her brown skin had taken on an ashy undertone.

"Rosa?" I reached out to touch her arm.

She started at the touch and stared at me, her eyes wide. "Alejandro is missing," she muttered. "He wasn't in his bed when my sister got up this morning. She's called the cops . . . but there are no leads, no sign of breaking and entering . . . " Her gaze had gone unfocused, staring off at some point in the distance. Blinking, she looked back at me again, some of the shock fading from her glazed eyes. "How did you know?"

"I . . . I told you, I had a dream . . . " I stammered.

"Did you cause this somehow, Tania? Is this your fault?" Her voice was now laced with hysteria, the shrill edge of it cutting through the noise of the market. Even though I knew it was shock and grief speaking, not reason, it stung. Rosa knew me, she trusted me, and she was always kind to me. People from the other stalls were starting to turn and stare, whispering to each other.

"No, Rosa, I would never." My eyes welled up with tears. The sting of disappointment and fear was all the more bitter for being on the heels of relief. I was *so* tired. I thought we'd avoided disaster. But of course not. "I'm so sorry. I don't know why this happened. But I promise, I didn't cause it." Even as I said it, I felt a little self-doubt burrowing in my heart. Maybe I had caused it somehow? Maybe this was *all* my fault. I sniffled and rubbed my hands over my grainy eyes and through my matted hair. I probably didn't look particularly sane at the moment.

Lost in emotion, I just about jumped out of my skin when a security guard clamped a hand down on my shoulder with a little too much force.

"Is everything okay here, ma'am?" he asked, looking at Rosa. He acted like I wasn't there, even as he was very much invading my personal space.

Rosa leaned back on her heels and took a deep breath in, wiping her eyes with her palm. "No, sir. We're fine. I just got some bad news. She's a friend."

The guard hesitated, loosening his grip but not letting go, and looked at me as though I were forcing her to say that. "Are you sure?"

"Yes, yes, I'm fine." She forced a tiny smile at the guard. It wasn't very convincing matched with her shaky voice, but I had to give her big points for effort.

Looking between us, he took in our mutual distress, his eyes lingering on my rumpled clothes and tangled hair. "All the same, I think it's best for her to leave. She's causing a scene and disrupting the other vendors."

I had stayed silent—barring the sniffles—thus far, but I couldn't take that one lying down. I gave him a dirty look and tried to wriggle away. "I was just trying to help! Her nephew—"

"That's enough from you," he growled. He turned on his heel, dragging me away. Trying not to stumble, I turned to look at Rosa, still standing shell-shocked by that godforsaken pile of potatoes. I noticed, for the first time, the small crowd of people who had gathered around, staring and whispering at the whole spectacle.

"Rosa!" I yelled back at her. I knew I wasn't helping things, but it was so important to me that she knew I didn't have anything to do with this. "I promise, this wasn't my fault! I didn't do this. If I can do something to help, I will!"

The guard shook me by the shoulders and shoved me in front of him, a nightstick jabbed in my ribs to keep me from turning around again. He took the longest path to the exit, frog-marching me through as an example of what happens when you misbehave. We must have passed every damn vendor in the place, who either looked on with obvious curiosity or made no eye contact whatsoever and pretended it wasn't happening. We passed a few of my neighbors, too, who averted their eyes, making it clear they had no connection to me, the troublemaker. I couldn't blame them. I was probably going to get a hard time from the guards for a while after this. If my neighbors could avoid that fallout, they should.

As luck would have it, right as we got to the gate, we passed the old Bible-thumper from the previous weekend, who appeared to be looking for another pot to stir. Here you go, lady: trouble at your feet, wrapped up with a bow. She surveyed me with glee, looked at the guard, and all but spat at me as she spoke.

"If something bad happened, this one caused it. I'm telling you. She's worse than most of them." And then, the crazy old bat *actually* spat at me. Luckily, I dodged it. Less luckily, that meant it landed on the guard's chest, who looked at me with disgust and shoved me through the gate. I didn't know how he could blame me; I wasn't the one spitting people in public like an ill-tempered llama.

"Don't come back this weekend!" he yelled after me.

I staggered into the nearest alley, trying to regain my balance from his rough push, and leaned against the cool bricks to collect my thoughts. My visit had pretty much confirmed the worst-case scenario. I trudged home, feeling defeat at the pit of my stomach. Alejandro *had* been taken. My dreams were definitely *not* just dreams.

My middle school math teacher, Mrs. Price, was whispering at the back of my head that technically, it took three times to make a pattern. There was no way I was going to sit around and wait for number three. Besides, I'd had three dreams. Chances were, the first dream had involved a kidnapping, too. I just lacked enough information about the kid to figure out who he or she was.

Shoulders slumped, I kept my eyes fixed to the ground as I marched home. Somehow, I didn't walk into anyone; everyone I met on the pothole-ridden pathways gave me a wide berth. Word traveled fast around here. By dinnertime, everyone this side of the fence and some on the other side would know about the show at the market.

Once I got home, it was obvious in one glance that Logan still hadn't come home. If he'd returned this late, he would have made some food before heading to bed. A glance inside his bedroom confirmed my suspicion. I started some coffee and scrounged around for something light to eat before I passed out from hypoglycemia and stress. We didn't have a whole lot of food on hand, so I settled on an apple. Note to self: next time, get your groceries *before* dropping a bomb about psychic kidnapping dreams.

I sat at the table, crunching on the apple and waiting for the coffee to brew. What was I supposed to do now? I was pondering my next steps when Logan burst through the door, humming a jaunty tune. I eyed him as he surveyed the room, clearly hoping the coffee was ready to drink (it wasn't).

"Why hel-loooo there, roomie!" he chirped. Mouth full of apple, I didn't even reply, just gave him a "what the hell are you doing" look. He answered the unspoken question. "I did *extraordinarily* well at the poker game last night—even for me. And not to kiss and tell, but there was a handsome gentleman at the event who was . . . how would you say it . . . definitely digging my chili." He waggled his eyebrows for emphasis.

I snorted despite my foul mood. When Logan was feeling perky, you couldn't help but feel a little bit better. Given that my usual response would have been a high five or actual laughter, he stopped skipping around the room to look at me. He took in my bedhead, the purple rings under my eyes, my messy outfit, and the overall general frowniness.

"I hate to say this twice in one week, but you look like something the cat dragged in. From hell."

I rolled my eyes and got up to throw away the apple core. "Not without reason. Talk about a shitty night and morning." As I poured the coffee, I glanced over my shoulder to see that he'd stolen my seat and was motioning for me to give him my mug. I scrunched my nose but relented, then poured a new cup for myself. "You know those dreams? The ones I'd had last week that you got all pissy about?"

He murmured an "mm-hm" that mingled with a casual slurp of coffee, not bothering to disagree with my assessment of his reaction.

"I hadn't had one all week," I continued. "I don't know if it's because my sleep schedule was off, or what. But I had one last night. Except it was . . . more real. The other dreams had felt a little muted, but this one . . . I could feel the snow. And I saw the woman. And the kid—it was Alejandro, Rosa's nephew. The boy I met last weekend."

He nodded, his grin disappearing.

"I woke up. Totally freaked out, of course. I mean, my pants were still wet from the snow. It was the weirdest thing . . . so I went to the farmer's market to see if Alejandro was okay. At first, Rosa said everything was fine. Then she got a call from her sister and learned that he's missing. There were no signs of a break-in or theft or anything, just . . . an empty bed. Rosa was pretty distraught . . . asked if maybe I caused it."

I paused for a moment, trying to keep the tears pricking my eyes at bay. Going over it out loud with Logan brought me right back to Rosa's face going gray with fear. I regained control and pressed on. "She calmed down some, but not before a guard saw the commotion and decided to intervene. The guy did everything but haul me out in handcuffs. In front of everyone, including that awful woman from last week, who caused another big scene. He told me not to come back this weekend."

I took a deep breath, waiting for him to react. In turn, he seemed to be waiting for my reaction. I felt pretty much reacted out, drained hollow from the last few hours. After a beat of silence, I added, "Logan, I know you said it was nothing, but it's obvious now that it's not. I'm the only one who's seen this kidnapper's face. I have to do something." Desperation entered my voice, even as I tried to keep it out. "I have to at least *try*."

He sat up a little straighter and set down his coffee. "You saw her face? Not from an angle like before?" I nodded, my face half-buried in the coffee mug. "What did she look like? Tell me everything you remember."

"She was gorgeous, but in kind of a creepy way. Like, she didn't look human. Not just model pretty, like you, but the next level after that. Some uncanny valley shit or something, like airbrushed photos in real life." I sighed and stared at the wall, willing myself to remember every detail. "She has a pointy chin and a really straight nose. Cheekbones you could cut glass on. Silvery-blonde hair and pale, like I said before. Her eyebrows are as light as her hair, and her eyes are ice blue." I shuddered and broke off my trip down memory lane to gauge Logan's reaction. I knew he wasn't going to be thrilled that we were discussing this again, but I wasn't quite prepared for how he did react. His white-knuckled hands gripped the table so hard it was creaking in protest, his lips were a thin line, and his jaw was clenched, making the veins on his neck stand out. "Uh, Logan? Are you okay?"

He growled through clenched teeth, staring straight ahead, his words short and sharp. "No. I'm really, really not."

I walked over and, after a moment's hesitation, reached out a hand to rest it on his shoulder. He flinched a little, but let it stay there. "What's the matter?"

Turning his face to me, he continued, eyes still distant and not meeting my own. "I know who the kidnapper is." My jaw dropped as he took a long breath in, nostrils flaring, and continued, "She didn't look human because she's not human. She's my sister."

I sat down on the floor so hard I almost dumped my coffee all over the tiles, trying to process this information. Logan's sister? How could I see her? Why would she be taking children? None of this made it out of my mouth, though. Instead, I just went, "Uh . . . "

Logan sighed and plunked his face down in his hands, palms pressed hard into his eyes. "I thought she might have something to do with it after our conversation the other day. It sounds up her alley—dangerous and wrong. But I didn't want it to be her, Tania. I just . . . I didn't." He sighed again, the huff of breath dampened by his hands. "That's why I got angry and blew you off." He lifted his face and finally looked at me, his green eyes now brimming with tears. "I'm sorry."

I broke the silence with a big swig of coffee. "Wow."

"Yeah."

I thought for a second, turning things over in my head. "Does this mean you know how to get the kids back?"

He shook his head. "I will give a big, emphatic *no* to that. You don't know her, Tania. If she's taking kids . . . there's a reason. There's some kind of plan involved. And she is ruthless. If something messes with her plans, if someone gets in her way . . . she'll kill them. No hesitation."

I leaned against him, still on the floor, trying to be reassuring, though I was scared and uncertain myself. "She sounds scary. But . . . if someone is taking children—and took Alejandro—I have to do something if I can. If nothing else, I need to figure out if I *can* do something."

He was silent for a moment, then stood and held out a hand to help me up. I brushed off my pants, and when I looked up at him, he was staring at me. He placed one hand on my shoulder and the other underneath my chin, tilting my face up, forcing me to make a bordering-on-uncomfortable amount of eye contact.

"Tania. I understand you want to help. But you have to trust me on this. You have to." His voice was even, every syllable weighted with a hopeless certainty I'd never heard before. "You can't go head-to-head with her and win. You can*not*. She had my boyfriend killed in front of me to gain political power. She will not think twice about doing the same to you." Exhaling, he dropped his hands to his sides, where they twitched with anxiety. "This upsets me, too, but if you're going to commit suicide by going after her, I'm not going to help. She's done enough damage to me without watching her hurt you, too."

I opened my mouth to argue, but he turned around and walked into his room, shutting the door. Not slamming it, not being dramatic for the sake of it, just refusing to engage. I stared at his door for a second, mouth opening and closing with no noise coming out, before I deflated into the chair. I rested my head on the table, finding the flat pressure somehow reassuring in its consistency. I felt like I had spent way too much time in this position lately.

Our mystery kidnapper was Logan's sister, a bona fide

sociopath by all accounts, and she was . . . what? Taking the kids to elf land for fun and games? Somehow, I didn't think so. If she was willing to be that horrible to her own brother, her own flesh and blood, what was she capable of doing to those innocent children? I shivered at the thought. Logan might not be willing to help, at least not right now. Given their history, that was understandable. It was obvious how much pain she'd caused him, and I didn't want to put my best friend in harm's way.

But that didn't mean I could just sit by and let this happen. Even if it *was* suicide to take action, I'd go crazy if I kept having these vision-dreams of kidnapped children and didn't do something. I'd never be able to sleep again.

Where did that leave me? If I was going to fight back, or even just save the kids, I'd have to do it on her turf. And that meant going through the Slip. To Logan's world. If that was even possible, it was going to be a lot of hard, hazardous work. I sighed and stood up, running my hands through my hair in a self-soothing effort at smoothing it. It might be a stupid plan, but I knew it was the only right one. Time to get to work.

# CHAPTER SEVEN

was sitting on the roof of an abandoned apartment building, bored out of my mind and freezing my ass off. Casing a joint was mind-numbingly dull. It wasn't hard to remember why it'd been years since I'd bothered to do it. Usually, I'd just use my trademark combination of glamour and the occasional well-placed boot heel to get in and out of a place. Given that armed guards patrolled the Slip at all times of day and night, I figured it might be better to have a plan coming in.

It was in the center of the city quarantine. The theory being, keep it as far away from the normal people as possible, in case it started emitting radiation or something. Back when the portals first showed up, there was a big radiation scare. After extensive testing, scientists concluded we weren't all going to sprout a fifth limb or start growing tumors. But science has never been particularly effective at calming hysteria, and their findings didn't stop the mass exodus from Slip cities for a few years.

The building I'd chosen as a lookout was an old, dilapidated structure, the closest I could get to the Slip. The industrial lighting illuminated the scene as bright as day, so at least I could see what was going on. As far as I could tell, there was only one entrance in the chain-link fence around the perimeter. There were two guards stationed at it, who appeared to be working six-hour shifts. Another guard patrolled the perimeter with a dog, completing a round every thirty minutes or so. That'd be a problem, because animals tended to get twitchy around the Marked.

The building they were guarding was squat and gray, resembling nothing more than a large storm shelter. No windows, and only one door with two guards stationed in front of it. Those appeared to also work six-hour shifts, but their shift changed halfway through the *other* guards' shifts. That meant there wouldn't be one massive shift-change, leaving the entrance vulnerable. Between the building and the fence entrance was a barren courtyard—no trees or grass, or even a sidewalk. Just packed dirt.

The inside layout was anyone's best guess. Ideally, I'd be able to impersonate a guard, get inside, check out the layout, and then leave before returning for the real deal. I'd be a lot more prepared that way. And if something went sideways . . . on the bright side, at least I'd be dog food before I'd ever have to worry about Logan's sister.

I could stick around and keep scoping things out, but I'd already been sitting here a solid chunk of the evening and well into the night. I'd learned all I could for now, and my numb fingers were begging to be wrapped around a warm mug of tea. I stood up and rubbed my tingling legs before making my way down the rusted fire escape. Traversing the alleyways at night here was always a crapshoot. You could find yourself in blissful solitude the whole way home. You could run into a friendly face. A lot of us were night owls, after all, since we tended to pick up whatever work we could find (and a lot of that type of work was at night). Or you could run into a junkie (or a drug dealer) that wasn't as nice as a Marked, and be a whole lot worse for wear afterward.

Lucky for me, I made it home in one piece with no awkward encounters. Logan was still out on his night's work, saving me from answering any awkward questions about how I'd spent my night. I brewed that much-needed mug of tea, warming my hands over the oven as the water heated up, and tumbled into bed after drinking it. I was so tired, I almost forgot to kick off my shoes and pants before I passed out. My last thoughts were about which guard to impersonate tomorrow. One step at a time.

The sound of a door slamming startled me into a state of semiawareness early the next morning. I assumed Logan had come home and was a little overzealous in closing the door—another good night, perhaps. I rolled over, pulled the blankets high above my head, and started to descend back into warm slumber. But instead of fading footsteps, I heard someone in my room, followed by an insistent shaking of my shoulder.

"Tania!" Logan hissed, whispering for some reason. "Tania, wake up!"

"Mmmffff. G'way," I mumbled into my pillow as I tried to wriggle from his grasp.

"I can't go away," he replied, still shaking me. "You need to get up. You've got to hide."

I threw off the blanket and glared at him, still bleary from sleep. "What? Are you drunk?" I shook my head, rubbing my eyes. "What time is it?"

He glanced behind him, like he expected the boogeyman to jump through the door at any given moment. "I don't know. Seven? Eight? Maybe a little later." He hooked his arms under mine and pulled me to my feet, then handed me my pants. "Here. Put these on."

I took them out of reflex. But instead of pulling them on, I stared at them, then looked at him and back. I'd woken up enough to wonder what the hell was going on, and I wasn't especially amused at this turn of events. "Logan. I am not getting out of bed at ass o'clock on a Sunday morning until you tell me what is going on." I crossed my arms over the pants and glared at him.

He gave an exasperated sigh and started chattering at breakneck speed, pacing around my room. "Fine. I was on my way back from the poker game, as usual, and saw a crowd of people outside the quarantine. Apparently that woman you saw yesterday is some kind of anti-Marked activist and told people stories about a Marked kidnapper. Turns out, it's more than just three or four kids. Kids from the surrounding neighborhoods have been going missing for a few weeks. She saw the scene yesterday and got nosy about what happened. When she found out, she rounded up a bunch of crazies to picket against the 'Marked menace.'"

He took a deep breath in, pausing, and then jumped back into the rush of words. "I overheard some guards on the way here. They're coming to interrogate you, Tania. They think you might have something to do with these kidnappings. You were asking questions about that kid, and you knew about Alejandro before anyone else." He stopped pacing to look at me, drumming his fingers on his thigh in agitation, then shook his head. Concern and fear were all over his face. "Given how they treated you when you were trying to *help*, I'm scared about what they'll do when they've got a frothed-up mob at their back. So." He pulled my arms out, picked up my pants, and pressed them into my hands again. "Get dressed. We're leaving."

I pulled the pants on in a daze. Here I'd thought things couldn't get a whole lot worse. How did they even figure that I would have done something so awful? If I were the kidnapper, I wouldn't be trying to help. I rummaged through my laundry pile at the foot of the bed, put on my leather jacket, and jammed my boots on, almost putting them on the wrong feet in my rush. Meanwhile, Logan continued to pace around the room in a panic.

"Should I take anything else? Is this a . . . temporary thing or . . . ?"

Logan shook his head. "I don't know, Tania. I don't think we have time. We've got to get you someplace else, right now, before—" A loud knock at the door cut him short. We looked at each other, terrified. He bit his lip and pressed his palms to the sides of his head. "Okay. Here's what we're going to do. Get in that closet"—he grabbed me by the shoulders and steered me toward it—"and do the best 'I'm not here' glamour you've got." He looked around the room. "This room should be empty. Make the room look empty, okay?" The front door rattled on its hinges under another round of thunderous knocks. Logan shoved me into the closet. "You can do this, Tania—we can do this together." The door shut, and I heard him walk off.

Crouching in the musty darkness, I closed my eyes and dipped deep into my energy reservoirs. I wasn't here. Nothing to see. The room was empty, with a few scattered papers on the floor. There wasn't even a door to the closet I was hiding in. If they couldn't see it, then they couldn't open it to look inside. I pictured it in my mind, crystal clear, but without getting hung up on the details. Getting too detailed was a rookie mistake. It was far better to give them a clear picture than an over-specific one. If you were clear enough with your intentions, *their* brain would fill in the gaps better than *you* ever could. I focused on the vision as hard as I'd ever focused on anything, even as I heard Logan's voice growing louder.

"Like I told you," he said, opening the door with a creak, "nobody's in here. This used to be Tania's room, but I haven't seen her for weeks. Maybe months. It's so sad, because we used to be just the *best* of friends . . . " He was laying it on thick. If I hadn't been focusing so hard on keeping up the glamour myself, I might have even been under his sway. One of the perks of being an elf is that you can make humans go dopey-stupid at any given point. It's not even a glamour so much as a weird voice-hypnosis thing.

"Yeah," I heard a guard reply, speaking in the distinctively slow way that someone hit with elf mojo does, "there's nobody here. Doesn't look like there has been for a while. Well, thanks for your help, Mr. . . . ?"

I could *hear* Logan's smile oozing charm. "Smith."

A second guard spoke up, also in a daze. "Yes. Mr. Smith. Thanks for your help. We'll report back to headquarters. Issue warrants. That sort of thing. Also, as a courtesy warning, the top brass might want to come by with dogs. It's typical in these sorts of cases. Just due process is all."

Logan sounded like he was smiling so hard his face might break. "Oh, I understand. But I think we all know that's not really necessary here. You said it yourself—nobody's been here for months. Right, fellas?"

The lack of verbal response meant, I could only assume, that they were both nodding in agreement. Not sure if that'd do any good once they got out of here and came out of their respective stupors, but it was a nice touch. The floor groaned as they left, my bedroom door closing behind them with a tiny click. I almost cried with relief, letting the glamour drop and leaning into the closet wall. I waited until I'd heard the front door shut and my bedroom door open again before I stuck my head out, looking for Logan.

"Are they gone?"

He nodded, glancing at the front door and chewing on his lip again. "They are. I might have overdone it. I'm worried they'll get back to their headquarters and realize they were being glamoured as soon as they sober up. Then they'll come back here, probably toting a pack of German Shepherds and armed to the teeth. We need a better plan."

I took a deep breath. "I think I have one, but I also don't think you're going to like it."

He looked at me with a mix of curiosity and skepticism, rubbing his chin. "I'm not a big fan of that preface, but we also haven't got a whole lot of options here. Let's hear it."

I left my hiding spot, pushing aside blankets on the bed to clear some sitting room, and motioned him over. I wasn't quite sure where to start, given how our conversation yesterday had ended. My nervous cough echoed in the tiny room.

"Well. I had already started to case the Slip facility last night, because I felt like I had to do something." The curiosity mixed with skepticism on his face was morphing into stubbornness, but I pressed on. "I mean, more planning would be ideal, a *lot* more planning, but they think I did it. You know how this works. I'll never get a fair trial. And if I could get the kids back, I think that'd clear my name," I finished as I ran out of breath, letting the hopeful words dangle in the air.

He sighed and shook his head. "I already told you, Tania . . . I want to help you. I do. You're the best friend I've ever had. But I can't go back there. If I did and got caught, I'd be killed. Probably tortured first, for a long time." He pinched the bridge of his nose between his fingers and screwed up his eyes. "And from our conversation yesterday, you already know that I'm not fond of the idea of you having anything to do with her. To be quite honest, I think your chances are a lot better over here than going head-to-head with Gwyneira." He shook his head again, shoulders slumped. "You can sway these humans, you can change your looks. Even if they post your face everywhere, you can still . . . live."

I pulled him to me and leaned my head on his shoulder, hugging him. "Logan, you know I love you, too. I won't make you go back there. I wouldn't do that. But I also don't want to be always on the run, glamouring all the time to survive, never getting a break. I'd be so exhausted, and you know I can't change my Mark. Maybe if mine were less visible, but it'd just be a matter of time. If going over there is a disaster . . . if I even *can* go over there . . . at least I tried. I have to try." He hugged me back and gave a weak nod. I untangled myself from our hug and stood up. "So, I guess I better start packing."

He stood up, too. "I'll help."

I snorted. "I know you think it's messy in here, Logan, but I only have the one small backpack. I think I can manage to put some pants and sweaters in it. I'm guessing it's cold over there, from my dreams."

He rolled his eyes. "No, dingbat. I mean, yes, it is cold, so bring some sweaters. And anything we have that'd keep well. Also, you wouldn't go wrong to pack some toilet paper. But also, I meant I'll help tonight, assuming you want to do it then. I'll help you get in the building. And then I'm out."

I nodded, throat tight, trying to maintain my composure. Logan was the longest-standing friend I'd ever had. Given his desire to escape this whole mess, even helping me out that much was a big deal. I dropped my eyes to the floor, because if I had to look at him, I *would* start crying.

The rest of the day was a blur. In a magnificent stroke of luck, the guards didn't come back with dogs. Maybe they were holding off until tomorrow. Logan went to the market for me in a more thorough disguise than usual. Rather than just changing his hair color, he made himself appear shorter and stockier, with buzzed hair and a ruddy complexion—still handsome, of course (you can't defy an elf's vanity). He got all the bread, apples, and cheese I could buy with my current funds. I, of course, couldn't go anywhere. I stayed in my bedroom and practiced squeezing everything possible into my backpack. Given the limited amount of clothing I could bring, it wasn't too hard. In went the sweater I wasn't wearing and the two pairs of jeans without holes, while the rest of the room was left for food. I practiced the packing technique my mom taught me, which could be summed up as, "Wear as much as possible, so you don't have to pack it." That meant I was wearing leggings with jeans over them, boots with my thickest, warmest pair of socks, a T-shirt, a sweater, my hoodie, and my leather jacket. Ten minutes of wearing that getup was enough to tell me I'd have to take it off until just before we left, unless I wanted to enter another world reeking of stale, nervous sweat.

After what felt like hours of pacing, rethinking every life choice I'd ever made, and hoping I wasn't making a massive mistake, Logan finally returned. Once I packed the food up, we talked strategy. Was it better to both go as guards, or have one person be a distraction while the other puts on a "nothing to see" glamour? The only dogs around would be patrolling the perimeter, so we needed to time it right and make sure that we weren't anywhere near them. After a lot of discussion, we had a decent plan, and even an okay backup plan. By that time, the red streaks of sunset had faded and night had settled in. Time to go.

As I finished bundling up again and strapped on my backpack, Logan gave me a once-over and smirked. "You look like an overstuffed turtle." I stuck my tongue out at him in reply.

We made our way to the building housing the Slip in relative silence. Even if I hadn't been too nervous to talk, we needed to be stealthy, which cut out the opportunity for idle chatter. We kept to the shadows as best we could, darting from one building to the next, closing in on our goal. Once we were a block away, we circled the building, looking for the weak spot we needed. And—there it was—the breaker box that controlled all the lights. It was off to the left of the fenced perimeter, on the outer wall of an empty apartment building.

I took a deep breath and, looking at Logan, broke the silence with a tense whisper. "You ready to do this? Once we start, there's not a lot of room for turning back."

Logan only hesitated for a split second before nodding. We locked eyes, and before I could turn away, he pulled me close for another hug, one so tight it knocked the air out of me. I didn't have a chance to catch my breath before he'd broken the hug, holding me out at arm's length to look me straight in the eye.

"I want you to be careful, Tania. Don't trust anyone. Be careful who you accept food or gifts from. And definitely, *definitely* don't tell anyone your name. I'll stick around here for a few weeks, okay? I'll be waiting for you for when you come back, with the kids." He gave me a wobbly smile that told me he thought I had a snowball's chance in hell of making it back with the kids in one piece, but that he'd be holding out for the slim chance I pulled it off.

I pushed him off me and ruffled his hair. "Hey, you be careful, too. Don't piss anyone off. I hear those poker guys can be real assholes." I gave him a grin, one almost as shaky as his. We placed our hands on the breaker box, inhaled in unison, and exhaled as we both flooded the box with energy at the same time. There was a loud snap-crackle-*pop*! And just like that, everything went pitch black.

I pulled my hood up before grabbing Logan's hand and giving it one last reassuring squeeze. Then I ran back toward the gates at breakneck speed, throwing up yet another "don't see me" glamour. As I neared the front gate, I could hear the guards shouting, irritated.

"Damn it, Clark! I thought you said you fixed the lights!"

"I did! I swear!" Clark replied with a nasal, defensive whine.

"Obviously not," snarled the first guard. "Now, go fix them for real." He sounded like a total beefcake, someone who could grind Logan or me to a bloody pulp if he had a mind to. I gulped and tried not to envision an angry guard turning us into magical hamburger as I watched for my moment from the shadows.

As Clark wandered off to fix the breaker, a bobbing flashlight beam in the dark, I circled around the entrance. I could hear a dog barking in the distance and crossed my fingers that it was far enough away it wouldn't pick up my scent. As my eyes adjusted to the dark, I could see that Beefcake was a dark outline, still at his station.

Right on cue, a slurred voice yelled from the murky black around the fence. "Hey! I think I'm lost!"

Beefcake swiveled, pulling out a flashlight and shining it around, trying to find the source of the noise. Logan, with short, dark hair and bright blue eyes, staggered out of the dark, three sheets to the wind by all appearances. When the guard turned toward Logan, I snuck behind him and slipped through the entrance. One entrance down.

I made my way across the courtyard, avoiding the shallow pools of light cast by the guards' flashlights. Right now, my main focus was on praying the lights wouldn't come back on anytime soon. As far as I could tell, Logan and I had done a number on the circuits, so I shouldn't have to worry. But if I found myself drowning in bright lights, surrounded by guards in a place I wasn't supposed to be, even the strongest "don't see me" glamour wouldn't do much good.

Hugging the side of the building, I could hear the guard arguing with Logan, who was playing the part of a friendly but lost, thick-as-a-brick drunk to a T. Any second now he'd be getting Beefcake to call for—

"Morgan! I need some backup here! Help me get this guy off our perimeter."

Whew. Morgan disappeared to join Beefcake, leaving a dark corner where she'd been standing, and only one guard on the entrance. I slipped into the shadow and drew it around me. The situation was so perfect (black outfit, darkness, distracted guard) that my charm was only drawing a tiny amount of energy. Which was great, since I might need that energy for later. I scooted closer to the door for a better look and saw, to my dismay, that it had a keypad. I knew it was a long shot, but I'd been gunning for an easy-to-pick lock or liftable keys dangling from a guard's pocket.

This was still workable, though. I refocused some of that saved energy and redirected it all toward making the remaining guard think he really had to pee. I mean, he had to go like he'd been in the car for six hours right after chugging a few gallons of coffee. It was a short wait in the shadows before he began shifting uncomfortably, then glanced around and rushed to the door. While he entered the entrance code, I snuck behind him and threw Logan a thumb's up. He was now busy staggering around with a guard on each side of him, trying to convince them he'd been invited to a rave at this location. I hoped he saw the signal and knew he could lay off, before the guards got tired of his schtick.

With that, I was in. After the guard peeled off down a side hallway to relieve himself, I took a few careful steps down what looked like the main hallway. The rundown state of the building surprised me. I knew these facilities didn't have much of a budget, between economic difficulties and other priorities. But I didn't expect it to be quite so shabby inside—flickering fluorescent lights, no modern tech that I could see, everything looking a little too beige.

Surprise aside, the more pressing issue was that the stark interior gave me no cover at all. My best bet was to find my target as fast as possible. If I got caught, I'd need some strong mojo to get out of it, and I was already starting to run low.

I dashed down the hallway, peeking in doors and looking around as I went. There were a few side hallways that led to utility closets and offices, but the place was mostly deserted at this hour, lucky for me. I hit the end of the hallway and came up short in front of a sturdy-looking metal door, with dings and scratches in its shiny surface. *Now* we were getting somewhere. I tried the handle and, to my surprise, found it open. I closed my eyes for a moment and put up a just-in-case last-ditch glamour, meant to transform my overstuffed turtleness into a guard in baggy gear. Taking a breath to steady my nerves, I stepped through the door to find myself in a lab.

Large-screen monitors, also beige and dated, lined the wall to my right. An exam table was to my left, and directly ahead were full-length glass windows. In the hushed silence, marred only by the whirring of the room's computers, I stepped forward, half amazed and half disappointed by what I saw. The Slip on the other side of the windows was . . . odd. It almost hurt my eyes to stare at it. It looked *wrong* in a way I couldn't quite articulate; it was clearly not of this world. It was like looking at the only crooked painting in an otherwise meticulous museum, jarring and a little unsettling.

But at the same time, it wasn't intimidating. For some reason, I had expected an epic display of size and grandeur.

Something that would inspire, awe, and terrify. This was just a six-foot-tall tear in reality. I walked the length of the room. From one angle, the tear looked about as wide as your average doorway and showcased a white-dusted forest—the same massive forest from my dreams, I assumed. From another angle, it looked like it was only a few inches wide. Pretty cool, and yet somehow anticlimactic.

"Huh," I murmured out loud to myself, wondering at the weirdness. I wasn't expecting a reply.

"What are you doing in here?" came a snotty voice behind me. I spun on my heel, heart in my throat. Judging by the scowl on the man's face, the lab had only been unoccupied for a moment while he had stepped out. He was standing right in front of the door, which he'd left ajar in his surprise, and was looking me up and down. Crossing his arms, he tapped his foot, accentuating his impatience with my cluelessness. "You know, only officers cleared for Level 6 should be in here. And you"—he surveyed me again—"are clearly not Level 6."

"Um . . . " I had no quips left, or good excuses. Giving him a controlling dose of persuasive glamour was out of the question—my energy reserves were nearing their end. I only saw one option. I was loathe to use it, because the results could be so unpredictable. But, between a rock and a hard place, what else could I do? Hoping it didn't go wildly awry, I added a small addition to my existing soldier-outfit glamour. As far as he could tell, I'd just given him a plausible explanation for my presence.

This was another trick I'd picked up on the streets. As with the empty bedroom earlier that day, I left it up to his brain to conjure up the details, rather than trying to do so myself. Doing things this way also took less energy, a bonus. Granted, I never knew what I'd just said to them, which could be a minor drawback.

The man's eyes glazed over, and he nodded, suddenly calm and reasonable. "Oh. Yes, yes, I see. You'll stay with me as long as you need to, so no intruders make it past the security breach. As a precaution. Okay."

My shoulders dropped with relief. Good thing he liked to hear the sound of his own voice. "Yes, that's correct. Now, where should I stand?"

He walked over to one of the monitors and rolled out a chair. "You don't have to stand, you can just sit over here with me. We both know it's all a formality, so you don't need to be all stiff. If I had a nickel for every time these lights went out, I wouldn't have to work here," he said with a laugh. "Just let me call Sophie so she can join us."

"Yeah, sure," I said as I sat next to him. I was still trying to figure out how I'd get inside to the Slip. It was a snag, but Dr. Lab Coat here wasn't calling the guards or shooting me, so I'd take it. I leaned back in the chair, waiting for him to press a button and call Sophie. Instead, he whistled so loud my ears rang.

Before I'd even had a chance to think, I clapped my hands over my ears and yelled, "What the hell was that?"

He quirked an eyebrow, like I'd just asked a stupid question. "I was calling Sophie. Like I said."

My eyes widened as I understood. I spun around and leapt out of my chair to shut the door before this situation got ugly. I was too late. A massive German Shepherd bounded in, running toward the scientist. Claws skittered on the tiles as it spotted me and stopped dead in its tracks. Sophie snarled, baring her teeth, her hackles raised as she advanced on me. Shit, shit, *shit*.

"No, Sophie, this is just . . . What did you say your name was again?" The scientist tried to calm her, arms out, speaking in soothing tones. I knew that was a futile effort—I'd been in this situation before and it would *not* end well. This called for drastic measures. The dog could tell I was Marked, and with her acting this way, it was only a matter of time until the scientist managed to break free of my glamour.

I dropped the previous guard glamour. Before the scientist had time to finish gasping with surprise, I'd grabbed the scariest glamour I could think of offhand: the creepy spider lady I'd used to scare the alleyway drunk a few weeks ago.

The scientist shrieked in a most unmanly fashion and backed himself into a corner. The dog kept growling, but only backed up a half step. I'd expected better results than that. I took an experimental step toward Sophie, hoping to scare her away. Instead, she responded by leaping at me with full force. I threw my arms up to shield my face, but Sophie was now in full-on attack mode. I bolted to the left and took a running leap onto an exam table, knocking over a stool in the process. It was only *just* high enough to keep the dog away from me, and in my eagerness to get away from her, I almost fell face-first off the other side of the table.

Now I was trapped on the table with the dog circling it, calculating her next move. I glanced across the room to check on the scientist. He was recovering from the shock of the scary glamour, standing up and making his way to the intercom on the wall by the door. This had gone a little off the rails. Just a *little*.

I was contemplating how to keep the scientist from getting to the intercom, without losing my limbs, when a blurred silhouette streaked into the room. Another whoosh, and the dog was gone—I could hear her muffled barks and growls. I had no idea what had just happened, but I wasn't going to let the opportunity pass. Taking advantage of his surprise, I jumped off the table, somehow managing to keep my footing, and pounced on the scientist, knocking him to the ground. I would have been successful in my attempt to subdue him, except he stumbled backward into a rolling chair when I jumped on him. We both turned ass over teakettle, hitting the ground with him on top of me, instead of the other way around. He grabbed my hair, lifting my head off the ground, and pulled back to slam it into the linoleum floor.

My fingers squeaked as I tried to get a grip on the floor and scoot away, even as I braced for impact. The impact didn't come, though. Instead, I heard a crack, and the scientist slumped down, limp and heavy, on top of me. I couldn't see anything and threw him off me in a panic, hoping that I wasn't about to be beaten unconscious, too. I stood up, fists out, ready to fight, and scanned the room to find . . . nobody.

"This is why I can't leave you alone."

I whirled around, looking for the source of the familiar voice. He was standing behind me with a smirk on his face. I tackled him with a hug.

"Logan! You are a lifesaver. A literal one." I beamed at him. He winked. "I know."

"We need to get the hell out of here." The two seconds we could spare for a happy reunion over with, I made my way to the only other door in the room and inspected it. "This door has a biometric key. Not just thumbprint, either—iris scan, too."

Logan walked over to the unconscious scientist and grabbed him under his arms, dragging him the few feet to the door. He double-checked the position to make sure he could get the scientist's thumb on the reader. Then he pried the scientist's right eye open and examined it. He closed his eyes for a second, hand still on the scientist. When he opened them again, his right eye was now . . . not his eye, but the scientist's. The whole process took about thirty seconds, after which he turned to give me a gloating expression.

I rolled my eyes. "Fine, you're supertalented, I could never shift just a tiny part of my body like that, blah blah blah. Let's go before someone hears that damn dog barking and comes in here with guns blazing."

He sniffed, not appreciating the sarcasm, then turned around to place the scientist's thumb on the reader and look at the iris scanner. The scientist was still out cold; I hoped Logan hadn't hit him hard enough to do permanent damage. The guy was just doing his job, after all.

The reader buzzed, and the camera whirred and beeped as it scanned Logan's eye. I pushed the green button next to the door. With a whoosh-click, the door unlocked. We glanced at each other as we stepped into the room. My nerves were kicking up again, and Logan looked like he was rethinking this idea. The room was bare, save for another wall of monitors, with a concrete floor. The cold air rushing through it caressed my face, a welcome change from the stale lab air. I circled the Slip, examining it up close. Logan was looking back and forth between the forest scene on the other side and me, fidgeting.

I bit my lip. "There's still time for you to get out, and I can take it from here. I appreciate the help, but . . . " I didn't know how to say that I didn't want my best friend to be a martyr on my behalf.

He shook his head. "No. This is something I *have* to do. I realized that by being terrified of Gwyneira, I'm still letting her control me. I have no idea if we have any chance of saving those kids. But not only is this the right thing to do, it's what I have to do, if I want to finally climb out from under her thumb."

I nodded and reached out to grab his hand. We walked around the Slip together until we faced the wide side of it. I looked at him, and he nodded in response to my unasked question. We took a deep breath in, then stepped into another world.

# CHAPTER EIGHT

tingled all over. My vision was dark, and I tried to gasp, but I had no control over my body. The world around me was a formless vacuum, and I was weightless in it for some amount of time I couldn't quite discern. It could have been five seconds, it could have been an hour. It's hard to tell how long has passed when it's just you, alone, in your head with no sensory input.

Everything slammed back into place, all at once, as my foot touched solid ground on the other side of the Slip. It felt like stepping off an escalator that was moving too fast. I staggered to regain my balance, windmilling my arms to keep from falling. Frigid air blasted my face; my breath hung suspended in front of me. My first thought as I took stock of my surroundings was, "Holy crap, it's cold." Within a few seconds, the initial shock wore off, and I realized with gratitude that it wasn't *that* cold, especially not with my layers upon layers of clothing.

My shock fading, I surveyed my new surroundings in wonder. This was the same forest from my dreams, no doubt. The trees were so wide, it'd take five or six people to reach all the way around them. And the snow was here, too, several inches deep. It was snowing at that exact moment, with huge, fluffy flakes drifting down to kiss my cheeks and melt on my eyelashes. The forest was in a deep hush, the kind I wasn't used to hearing (or not hearing, as it were). A silvery full moon hung low and bright, taking up a huge chunk of the star-sprinkled sky. The moonlight reflected off the snow, giving everything a white glow.

Put together, the whole effect created every fairy-tale forest you've ever read about. It was awe-inspiring. Catching my breath, I turned and realized Logan was standing a few feet away, watching my reaction.

"It is beautiful, isn't it?" he said with a smile.

I grinned back at him, relief and the scenic beauty making me giddy. "It is." I glanced behind us, at the Slip, where I could still see the lab on the other side. I shook my head to clear it as the worries set in again. "We need to get as far away from here as we can, though. I doubt they'll come after us, but we don't want to take that chance."

Logan nodded in agreement, then glanced at the sky again and spun in a slow circle, as though he were looking for landmarks. "It looks like it's the middle of the night, so we should walk until dawn and sleep during the day. We'll be safer that way." I didn't ask from what. Heaven knew I already had enough nightmare fuel at the moment. "The castle is this way, I think." He pointed through the woods and struck off, walking at a brisk pace.

I ran a few feet to catch up with him and then kept pace alongside him, having to walk at double time to keep up with his leggy gait. "So," I said, glancing sideways at him to see if I could gauge his reaction. "Back there in the lab. I've never seen you move that fast before. Is that a new thing?"

He looked up at the sky as we walked, his laughter echoing off the trees. "Oh, Tania. You've seen I'm going to say a little more than half of what I can do. So many of my abilities are overkill for your world. That particular trick is also a huge energy drain, so it's kind of a last resort. I had just enough juice left to do that partial shift and fool the biometrics scanner, but if I'd had to do a full body shift, we would have been SOL."

He looked from the treetops to me to give an appraising look before continuing. "We should talk more about energy and powers. You're going to find that you have a lot more energy to draw off of here. You'll be able to do things that might be difficult back home. You should practice on smaller stuff at first, just like when the Slip first happened. It'll be easier to lose control here. It might be worth it for me to train you on a few things or for us to practice together, when we get the chance. It's also likely that there are things you can do that you don't *know* you can do. Back there, we had to focus on just getting by, and that doesn't leave a lot of room for experimenting with your talents. Surviving here takes a lot more work than surviving there. We should try to test your real limits."

"Yeah," I panted. "That sounds like a good idea." I would have gone on talking, but slogging through the snow while keeping up with him was leaving me out of breath. I wanted to pester Logan with all sorts of questions about what else he could do, what he thought I could do, and why our skills came to us more easily here. It could wait until we had a few minutes to talk and I wasn't kicking myself for my lack of exercise. If only I'd jogged around the block now and then, I wouldn't be winded already. I was great at short-term sprints—getting out of bad situations often required it—but I already hated this. I put all my focus on following him, and we fell into a comfortable silence as we trekked through the woods.

Hours—and, I could only hope, several miles—later, the sun peeked its lonely head above the treetops. We took a break, leaning on one of the massive trees and enjoying the freshness of our surroundings. Icicles hanging from the branches glistened in answer to the sun's arrival, while the snowfall reflected the new light with an almost painful brightness. Once again, I found myself looking around, struck by the breathtaking beauty of it all.

"Things seem more real here somehow," I murmured, almost to myself. "Everything is way more vivid."

Logan grunted, pushing himself off of the tree to stretch. "It does that to you. Try not to get too enchanted with it. The more you focus on the beauty, the prettier it looks, the more it gets inside your head, and that makes it easier for . . . unsavory types to take advantage."

I nodded. "Are there any more ground rules I should know?"

"Good question. As long as you're with me, you should be pretty safe. It's good for you to know the basics, though. In general, don't tell anyone your name, and definitely not your full name. *Ever.* Knowing your name gives someone power over you. You could fight that power to some extent—we both know how strong willed you are." He paused to give me a smirk. "But it'd be better to avoid it from the get-go."

He continued stretching, bending over to touch the tips of his toes. "Be careful about accepting gifts—specifically food. That saying your people have, there's no such thing as a free lunch, applies here, too. Accepting a gift from someone, in most cases, puts you in their debt. You don't want to owe anyone here if you can help it. Speaking of food . . . " He gave my backpack a meaningful look. In response, I bent over and pulled out an apple for each of us.

Crunching on his, he sat back down against the tree and continued, "No names, don't accept gifts. We already talked about being careful with your talents until you adjust to the ease of things here. What else? I guess, in general, don't trust people. People here are devious, and they won't know what to make of you. For most of our history, the humans that made it over here were almost all under someone's glamour, or some poor sap that stumbled through a mound by accident. They'd try to find their way home again and eventually make it back, only to realize that several hundred years had passed." He stared at his apple core and shrugged before flicking it away. "Humans with powers are so, so rare. Or used to be. We'd maybe see one every five hundred years or so. Before I crossed over, I'd never seen one, just heard stories."

I went over his list of rules again in my head. No names, no gifts, don't trust anyone, and don't get taken in by the beauty of the place. That was easy enough to remember. As I finished my apple, Logan stood up and studied our surroundings. "Now that the sun's up, we can sleep for a few hours. It looks like it's dry under that tree there."

We walked toward the massive fir he'd pointed out, which was indeed free of snow near its base. I flopped down on a bed of pine needles and placed my backpack under my head, trying to ignore the pinecones poking into my back. Logan lay down next to me. He interlaced his fingers behind his head and stared up at the tree.

"Logan," I said, turning toward him. I might be about to get myself in big trouble, but I was curious enough to ask. "Despite everything, does it feel good to be home?"

He didn't look at me, but kept gazing up at the mosaic of needles, snow, and sunlight breaking through the forest canopy, his face expressionless. When he did reply, his words were measured and reflective. "Yeah, it kind of does."

I didn't have anything else to say, and I was too tired to talk, anyway. We'd been in constant motion for the last twenty-four hours, and now that we'd stopped, I was struggling to keep my eyes open. Even though I was lying on damp twigs and pokey fir needles, and even though I hated sleeping during the day, I was sound asleep in a few minutes.

Hours later, I sat up and rolled my head around, then rubbed my eyes. I realized with surprise that I didn't feel too awful, despite our less than five-star sleeping accommodations. Judging by the light, it was now mid- to late afternoon, which meant we'd got a solid seven or eight hours of sleep.

I twisted and turned, stretching out the stiffness from our long walk the night before. In the process of working out the kinks in my neck, I noticed Logan wasn't next to me anymore. There was a dent in the needles where he'd slept, but no sign of him. On high alert, I eased myself up, hearing a potential threat in every bit of birdsong or rustle of leaves.

I listened for a minute or so, frozen in place, until his voice drifted through the trees, quiet and without any hint of alarm or anger. I let myself relax a bit and circled the tree, figuring he was nearby. I yawned, covering my mouth with one hand and trying to tame my hair with the other. Now that I knew Logan wasn't in mortal danger, I was wishing for some better personal hygiene options—I was pretty sure I had morning breath from hell. I was still pondering my dire need for a toothbrush when I spotted Logan and stopped in my tracks.

Standing next to him was . . . I struggled for the right word . . . a woman. She was buck naked and didn't appear to be bothered by the cold. In place of skin, she had rough dark-brown bark. Her appearance did *not* leave a lot to the imagination, and I fought the urge to blush and avert my eyes. Round forest-green eyes looked out of a pixie-like face with a sharp chin, and her hair resembled nothing more than a mat of evergreen needles sticking out all over her head. She stood close to Logan, not even coming up to his shoulder—I guessed she was maybe five feet tall. Their conversation was in low tones, punctuated with the occasional urgent hand gesture, but I couldn't make any words out. As I approached, the conversation died and they both looked at me. "Uh, hi," I said, suddenly feeling like I had a spotlight on me.

The woman turned to Logan. "That's her?" she said, gesturing at me.

"Yes, that's her, and she has a name," I retorted, annoyed.

The strange woman spared a glance at me, unruffled by my snottiness, and came closer to examine me.

"Tania, don't be rude," Logan chided. "This is Rowan. She's a dryad."

*That* was the word I'd been looking for.

The dryad was still circling me. I didn't really like the way she was sizing me up, but if Logan was telling me not to be rude, there was a reason. "That's, uh, a tree spirit, right?"

She stopped evaluating me to put her hands on her hips and sniff. "To say 'tree spirit' is like calling you a"—she paused to think—"hairless monkey. It is technically accurate, but not quite polite. I am a tree spirit, but not just that. I guard this part of the woods." She motioned around us with one hand, the other still perched on her hip. "The creatures here are under my protection, as are all who pass through here." She glanced back at Logan, then returned her green gaze to me. "*If* I desire and allow them to do so, that is."

"Oh." I gulped. "Uh, do you . . . desire?"

Rowan blinked, then laughed, a sound that reminded me of rustling leaves mixed with birdsong.

Logan smiled and clapped me on the shoulder. "Rowan and I go way back, Tania. We can trust her. She's going to help us."

"Oh." I sighed with relief. "Well, Rowan, I'm sorry, I didn't mean to be rude. You're the first, uh, dryad I've ever met. But it is nice to meet you!" I stuck out my hand to shake hers, and she bent over to examine it as though I were handing her something. "Oh, uh, no, it's a . . . friendly custom where I'm from. You shake hands, like this." I demonstrated with Logan. She watched with her round eyes, then tossed me a bemused and slightly disdainful look that could only be described as catlike.

"Mm-hm. Well." She turned around and strode toward the tree where we'd slept. "Let's see how I can help you two." Her finger crooked, she gestured for us to join her. We moved closer, my curiosity piqued as to how she was going to help us. Once we were all standing at the base of the tree, Rowan placed a hand on it and leaned so close to the tree I thought she might kiss it. She whispered something that sounded like dry leaves in the wind and creaking branches. The tree shuddered, then groaned. I stepped back in shock as I realized that one of its larger branches, at least four feet wide, was bending down, giving us a leg up (or rather, a branch up) into the boughs of the fir.

Rowan and Logan didn't hesitate. They strode over to the branch and hopped on top of it, acting like it was the most natural thing in the world. Logan waved for me to do the same, saying, "Come on, Tania! Don't be scared. You'll love this. I promise." His eyes twinkled, but I couldn't tell if it was with mischief or enthusiasm. They were often the same with him, anyway.

Hesitant, I walked over to the branch and hoisted myself up onto it, far less gracefully than Logan and Rowan. The tree creaked again and we rose into the boughs. The branch continued to rise until it was stretching up at a forty-five-degree angle and rasping in a way that sounded painful. I expected it to stop, but it pushed on a little farther. Then, in another move I didn't expect, it tilted to one side. Logan and Rowan seemed to anticipate this and each took a smooth step onto the adjacent branch. As for me, I shrieked and stumbled onto the new branch with all the grace of a drunk partygoer.

Rowan's mouth twitched at the corners as she bit back a laugh. Logan didn't bother showing such restraint, laughing so hard I thought he might make himself sick. I shot him a dirty look as I brushed errant fir needles off my pants and shook them out of my hair.

"You could have warned me," I snapped. He shrugged at me through the waves of mirth.

"I apologize," said Rowan, sounding a little stiff, but not sarcastic. "I assumed you had traveled by tree before. If you have never done it, it can be a little disorienting. Are you all right?"

"Yes, thank you," I replied, surprised at, but grateful for, her politeness. "I'm fine. It just startled me. We don't have this method of travel where I'm from, so I've never done it. Which"—I glared at Logan again as he wiped a tear from his eye, still chortling—"he knew."

Rowan nodded, her face sympathetic. "Are you ready for the next part? There won't be any more surprises."

I almost gave her a thumbs-up, but thought better of it, nodding instead. She spoke aloud again to the tree, in that strange rustling, creaking language, and our current branch stretched upward. We climbed up and around the tree in a spiral and landed on a new branch, then that branch lifted us up and put us on another branch. The branches started getting thinner, though they were still wide enough to stand on without feeling too unsafe. And then the branch we were standing on didn't put us on a new one. It just lifted us up, and up, and up a tiny bit more. Our heads broke through the forest canopy, and we could see for miles.

I gasped, mouth hanging open. Off in the distance, purple-gray mountains cut through the horizon shrouded in mist. Below the mountains were rolling hills, dotted with shrubs, skeletal trees, and evergreens like our current perch. Those trees appeared to be smaller, more like normal trees. And around us, for miles in every direction, the sun glinted off crystal-tipped trees, making me feel like we were looking down on a palace of white and green.

"It's beautiful," I whispered. Out of the corner of my eye, I could see Rowan was practically preening from my reaction, soaking in the praise.

"Isn't it, though? I am a lucky dryad indeed to have stewardship of these lands."

Logan was also surveying the landscape, but with his eyes squinted in concentration instead of wide with awe. Turning to Rowan, he said, "Has the forest moved any closer to the castle since the last time I was here?"

She shook her head. "It's the same as it was before—the forest borders the farmlands, which go right up to the castle gate. The one change is that there's now an official roadway through the forest. You'll want to avoid it, though. There's a lot of traffic, most of it castle guards. I think you would be best off travelling parallel to the roadway. That way, you can follow it to the castle. You can sneak through the farmlands, or . . . " She paused, her brow furrowed in thought. "The forest is closer behind the castle, where the land isn't good for farming. You could circle around the farmlands and approach the castle from there, if you want to stay in the shelter of the forest." She shrugged. "We all know traveling through the forest comes with its own drawbacks, though it provides more cover than the farmlands."

Logan nodded, deep in thought. I was listening, but I was a little lost. Maybe I could get him to draw me a map later.

They discussed a few political changes—Lord Who-sy-Whatsits owns this fiefdom now, Lady So-and-So took control of that ford. These alliances were stronger, those were weaker. I knew I should listen, but I'd never had a head for political intrigue. Especially when it involved names without faces and an intricate, overlapping backstory that I knew nothing about. I tuned them out, looking at the landscape and trying to commit every detail to memory. Assuming I made it back home, I wanted to remember this view.

After a few more minutes of discussion, we started our trip back down, returning to the frosted forest floor. Logan and Rowan continued talking politics, while I checked on the supplies. The sun being up and shining prompted me to shed a layer of clothing, so I took off my hoodie and stuffed it into the backpack. I tore off a hunk of bread and nibbled on some cheese, taking the opportunity to eat a snack. By the time I finished, they were saying good-bye, and Logan even uttered a few words of her language. They touched each other's shoulders, then stepped back and bowed in what looked like a formal but genuine show of respect.

She turned to me with a small half smile. "Do whatever you can to keep Logan safe, please. We value him here."

I smiled back. "I value him, too, despite his awful sense of humor. I've got his back." She gave me a quizzical look. "Um. I mean, I'll help protect him, as he would and has protected me." She looked more satisfied with that and, after a moment of hesitation, stuck her hand out. I shook it, saying, "It was an honor and a pleasure to meet you, Rowan."

Giving me a small bow, she smiled before turning away. As she walked off into the surrounding trees, a curious thing happened. Some fifteen feet away, the air shimmered where she stood, and then—poof!—no more dryad. Maybe I could learn *that* trick.

I turned to Logan, who was staring at the spot where Rowan had disappeared, lost in thought. "So, which way are we heading and what's our plan?"

At hearing my voice, he snapped out of it. "I think Rowan's plan is best. We should find the road," he replied as we trekked through the snow. "Then we can check every mile or two to make sure we're still on course, but generally we should stay back in the woods. We shouldn't get lost, but stick with the route if we get"—he hesitated—"separated or something."

I knew he was thinking about what his sister would do if she found him, and I didn't want to give false reassurances. Instead, I asked, "How did you meet Rowan?"

"Oh, we've known each other since we were children. With elves in general, and especially with my family, each of us has an affinity for a particular element of nature. Not the four elements—earth, air, fire, water. It *can* be that simple, but it can also be an affinity for the mountains. Or the sea, as opposed to all bodies of water. Gwyneira's affinity is for water. I imagine that's why you saw her emerge from a lake. Since that's her natural strength, it's the easiest way for her to pass between the worlds. It helps that water has functioned as a way to pass between worlds since the beginning."

He waved a hand at our surroundings. "My affinity is for the forests. The animals that live here, the plants, the trees. My sister, for example, can't speak the dryad language. She might be able to develop a basic understanding of it after years and years of practice, but I picked it up in a few weeks." He stopped walking and cast his eyes around, looking for something. "Here, watch this."

He bent over and sifted through a bare patch of soggy dirt to pull out an acorn. He brushed away a few clumps of mud clinging to it and held it up for me to see. He then cupped his hands around it and, bringing it to his lips, whispered something I couldn't hear. A shimmering green light peeked out between his fingers, shining onto his face. His eyes glowed bright emerald in answer.

A few seconds passed before he pulled his hands away from his face and opened them. The acorn had sprouted, a tiny stalk stretching out of it with miniscule fuzzy green leaves waiting to unfurl. Threadlike white roots had wrapped themselves around Logan's middle finger. He stared at it for a moment, then placed his hand over it again. When he removed them, the acorn was back to being just an acorn. His eyes faded, returning to their normal shade of green.

"That was amazing," I breathed, eyes wide. "Can I do stuff like that?"

Logan shrugged. "I don't know. I don't know if the way our talents work is similar, if the Marked also have different affinities, or if you're all just sort of a . . . mishmash. Either way, we shouldn't experiment with that particular trick right now, given what I mentioned about things coming to you more easily here." He gave me a wry smile. "The first time I tried it, I couldn't control the energy at all. The tree was four feet tall before I managed to stop."

He wiped his hands on his pants and jerked his chin, indicating we should continue walking. I fell into step beside him, deep in thought. He hadn't been kidding when he said I only knew half of what he could do. And there might be more things that *I* could do, too.

"So," I mused, "hypothetically, what else can I do?"

He ran his hands through his hair, thinking. "All kinds of things. There's defensive magic—but that's never been my strong suit, so I can't teach you much of that. There's elemental or nature-based magic: starting or manipulating fires, freezing water, summoning the wind, changing the weather—although that one takes a lot of energy." He ticked each one off on his hand as he spoke. "And there's clairvoyance, where you can see things that are happening even if you aren't physically there." He glanced at me. "I bet you can do that, if you work at it. Often, those who have dreams like yours are clairvoyant."

I scrunched my nose in disgust. "I'd rather do something else. That sounds so late-night cable-TV dial-a-minute psychic."

Logan's laugh echoed through the quiet forest. "It's not my fault the human word for it sounds hokey. Don't shoot the messenger. Anyway, it can come in handy, especially if you hone it."

"Do glamouring or shifting fall under a particular affinity?"

Logan shook his head. "Not for us, anyway. All elves can do that sort of thing. As far as actual shifting goes, full-body shifting into animals is an uncommon ability. But being able to shapeshift into another person is the norm."

I thought about it for a second. "So . . . how do you ever know who you're talking to?"

He shrugged again, like the answer was obvious. "We have a formal culture, with strict rules that we stick to. Using shifting to impersonate someone else is considered to be in bad taste, even if you do it as a joke. And we can see right through each others' glamours; trying to glamour someone is . . . what's the best way to put it? It's an insult. You're saying you don't think they're smart or aware enough to see what you're doing.

It works on non-elf people—I could have glamoured Rowan, if I wanted to—but most elves will see right through it."

I wanted to get all the information I could while Logan was feeling chatty. "And when you said earlier that things would be easier for me here, what did you mean? Why does that happen?"

"If your talents are anything like ours, they come from something in the fabric of reality. At least, the fabric of reality here." He waved a hand at our surroundings. "Their origin is quite a hot topic of discussion among philosophers and scholars. But the gist of it is that here, you're closer to the source of your powers. Why not try something and see if I'm right?"

I stopped and looked at my hand, thinking back to the incident with the guards a few days ago. Logan had paused a few feet ahead and was giving me an "I'm being very patient and hope you appreciate it" look.

Taking a deep breath, I focused, aiming to shift my hand into a hooked hand with sharp talons. He was right—I finished in a matter of seconds. Back home, pulling from my energy felt like drilling a hole into a deep reservoir. Once I got there, the energy was easy to use and there was plenty of it, but it took concentrated work to tap it. This was like skimming water off a lake. Effortless. I shifted my hand back to normal and turned it over, looking at it.

"You're right." I grinned, excited at the possibilities. "Once we stop for the night, I'm going to have to play with this some more."

He winked at me. "I usually am right."

We continued walking in peaceful silence, Logan seeming content to watch our surroundings as we meandered along. For my part, I was mulling over everything I'd learned in the last few days. There was one thing I couldn't help returning to over and over again. I wasn't eager to bring it up, but it was important to know if I was going to survive this little adventure.

"Logan?"

He didn't even look at me as we continued weaving our way through the snowy trees. "Mm-hm?"

"How did Gwyneira turn bad? I mean . . . was she always like that, or did something trigger her . . . ?" I didn't know where else to go with my questions, so I just trailed off and let them hang.

Logan still didn't look at me, but he paused for a moment, staring into the darkening gaps between the trees. At least he didn't look angry. Thoughtful and sad, but not furious with me for asking. I thought he was going to ignore the questions, but after a long pause, he spoke.

"She wasn't always like that." Staring at the ground, he started forward again. I followed suit, trailing behind a bit, trying not to crowd him but hanging on every word. "We used to be close. She's not much younger than me. The equivalent in human years would be two or three years. She saved me from drowning once. If that had happened later, I doubt she would have done the same thing."

Silence sank in around us again. I didn't know if I should prod him or not. After a few moments of silence, I decided a prompting question was worth the risk. "What happened?"

Sighing, he shook his head. "The way things work here, each kingdom operates almost entirely independent of the others. There's a meeting of rulers of the kingdoms every hundred years or so. Grievances with other rulers or their policies are aired, and the rulers are held accountable for their actions by the other rulers. Sort of like a high council. Anyway, since I was the eldest, I was in line for the throne. I was never much interested in politics, though, and found a lot of the strategy aspects of it boring. Somewhere around her coming of age,

Gwyneira got it in her head that she would be a better ruler than I would." His shoulders slumped. "And maybe she was right. As I began to get more involved in governing our kingdom, her resentment grew. She barely talked to me, except to criticize my decisions.

"There would have been ways to handle it. I guess she didn't think the 'proper channels' would do much to help her cause, because I was popular both at court and with the citizens. So she tried to bring me down with personal attacks instead." He barked a sad laugh. "I say 'try,' but obviously it worked. Over time, she planted the idea among the advisors to the throne that I was unfit to rule, that I would never father children . . . you get the drift. When our father died, she seized her opportunity. You pretty much know the rest."

I was glad I'd asked—knowing her backstory could come in handy. I did wish there wasn't so much pain in his voice, though. I reached out and squeezed his hand in what I hoped was a reassuring way. Giving me a small smile, he squeezed back before dropping his hand away.

By this point, night had well and truly fallen. I looked up at the same view as the night before, including the enormous full moon. My curiosity piqued, I seized the change of subject.

"Are there normal moon cycles here?"

"Not exactly. Sometimes the full moon lasts three days, sometimes a week, sometimes a month, sometimes more. The moon goes through the same phases you're familiar with, but it does so on its own sweet time."

A strange keening in the distance interrupted my one-sided staring contest with the moon. I thought maybe I was the only one that had heard it. Logan, however, had frozen in his tracks, his head cocked to one side.

"Did you—"

He cut me off with a sharp shushing gesture. The noise

sounded again, closer. He glanced around, drawing in air between his teeth in a distressed hiss.

I tried not to let any fear seep into my voice. "Logan?"

"We need to move." Offering no explanation, he took off at a sprint. I hustled to keep up. As I ran after him, the noise sounded yet again. As it moved closer, I could make out a variety of other sounds. A chorus of wails, yips, and howls intertwined with the keening, and a deep thundering rumbled underneath it all. I could feel it reverberating in my lungs, like being too close to the speakers at a concert. At the same time, the wind kicked up, adding its own wailing into the mix, forcing the trees around us to join the cacophony with grinding creaks and moans.

I panted as I ran, my pulse pounding in my ears, goosebumps popping up all over my body, and cold sweat pooling in the small of my back. In the dark, I stumbled, tripping over a root. I tried to stay on my feet, but instead fell face-first into the snow. Clumsy with adrenaline, I was struggling to stand up when Logan grabbed me and pulled me aside, around a tree—and then into it.

We crouched inside a hollow oak tree, a space as big as our kitchen back home. Shivering and struggling to breathe, I whispered, "Logan, what the hell is going on?"

We listened to the rising orchestra. He peered out. "Have you heard of the Wild Hunt?"

I tore a hand through my hair, trying to think. "No, I don't think so."

"Short version: I think they're on our trail. If they catch us—well, the chances of your surviving are slim to none. If you did, you'd be . . . ah, not the same. They're not very nice to people who aren't from here. I'd survive, but who knows what they'd do to me." He had to raise his voice to be heard, and even so, I could hardly hear him. The wind kicked up with renewed force, as though trying to bring the damn tree down around us. I could feel the tree shuddering in response.

"Wh-what do we do?"

He crossed the space between us in a heartbeat. "They're circling in." Grabbing my hands, he looked me in the eyes. "Tania. I have to lead them away. They'll find us, now that they're on our scent. They won't be able to catch me. I'll find you again tomorrow, okay?"

"No . . . no, I can go with you, we can lose them together," I pleaded, pulling my hands out of his to clutch at his shirt, trying to keep him in place. "Don't leave me here alone."

"You won't be able to keep up. Remember me back there in the lab?" He tried to keep his tone light and teasing, but I could tell he was serious. Another wail sounded, and this time it was right outside the tree. He glanced at the entrance, then kissed me on the forehead and hugged me tight. "You'll be fine. Keep experimenting—find out what you can do. You haven't even scratched the surface yet, I bet. I'm not friends with talentless losers." He grinned and I sniffled in return, afraid to talk because I knew I'd start crying. "If I don't come back . . . If I don't find you tomorrow, try to find the White Woman of the Forest, Tania. She's powerful, and she'll help. She'll know I sent you. Promise me you'll look for her, okay?"

I nodded through the haze of tears clouding my vision. "I promise." He stood back and my arms dropped to my side. "Be safe," I choked out.

He nodded and gave me another grin. "You, too. Don't do anything I wouldn't do." And then, in a blur, he was gone, in the same second the noise kicked to a fever pitch, so loud I couldn't hear myself think. I stared at the spot where my only friend in the world had just stood, then crouched in the corner. Trying to stay as quiet as possible, I listened as the howls and the accompanying thunder and wind retreated. The previous wintry stillness returned. No longer worried about alerting anyone to my presence, I crouched in the corner and sobbed until I fell asleep.

# CHAPTER NINE

The next morning, I woke up curled on my side. For a second, I thought I was back home. The inside of the tree was warm and dry, nest-like, and my brain was still foggy with sleep. That illusion disappeared as soon as I sat up and looked around.

My eyes were dry and my face tight with old tears. I brushed myself off as best I could—just because it was comfortable didn't mean it was clean—and rustled around in my backpack, looking for food. There wasn't a lot left. I ate one of the two apples left and all the bread, figuring that it was okay to eat more since I'd be walking all day. Judging from the light peeking into the little wooden cavern, I hadn't slept as late as we had the day before.

I stretched, slung the backpack over my shoulders, and walked out, checking to make sure I wasn't surrounded by orcs or whatever. I felt exposed, frustrated, exhausted, and still a little hungry after my meager breakfast. It was only when I started to walk that I realized I didn't know where to go. I had no idea where the road was, and our run through the woods last night had me all turned around. Maybe I shouldn't even look for the road anymore, since Logan had told me to find the White Woman, whoever that was.

Squeezing my eyes shut, I fought back a wave of tears. "Logan wouldn't have left you if he didn't think you could fend for yourself," I muttered. "Prove him right. Get it together." I shook myself off and smoothed my hair, regaining composure. Trying to guess from the sun's position, I picked a direction that I thought was the same way we'd been going, before the Hunt intervened. If I was supposed to find this White Woman, maybe someone who knew how to reach her would be on the road. If not, I could at least work my way closer to the castle in the meantime and figure out what to do next.

Without Logan's company, it wasn't long before I found myself bored out of my ever-loving skull. The forest was pretty, but it seemed to suspiciously lack wildlife. Thinking on it, I wasn't sure I'd actually seen another living creature besides Rowan since we'd arrived. There was birdsong and the occasional rustling of underbrush, but that was about it.

After hours and hours of walking, my feet ached and my eyes were gritty, but I was determined to make some progress today. Logan had put himself in harm's way—*again*—to help me out, and I didn't want to let him down. To occupy my mind, I counted my footsteps. I lost count once I got to five hundred. Then I counted the trees, but that game lost its amusement after fifty or so. As a last resort, I tried to identify the trees I was passing. I'd never been much for the outdoors, so that game got old after I couldn't figure out what other types of evergreen existed besides fir and pine. Or were fir and pine the same thing?

Somewhere in the midst of these tree-related musings, my

stomach snarled at me, reminding me to stop and eat. Those hours of walking had taken their toll. I dug out the last apple and munched while I continued wandering, the noise echoing through the quiet woods. I was now officially out of food, and it looked like it was only a little past noon. Too bad we hadn't had more food to pack.

A few hours later, as the shadows lengthened and the sun brushed the horizon, the gnawing hunger was back, and worse. Thinking maybe I could forage up a snack, I took a closer look at the trees as I passed them. One tree, a knotty, sprawling thing with low-hanging branches and thick needles, was covered in red berries. I grabbed a handful and stared down at them, weighing my options. Maybe I could just eat one, or half of one, and see if it affected me before I ate the rest? Or maybe I should just keep going and wait until I was ravenous before making any rash decisions. Then again, I reasoned with myself, by the time I was *that* hungry, I probably wouldn't be thinking straight. I might not be so keen on the "testing and waiting several hours" strategy, then.

I had just decided that I was going to try one of them when a male voice crept up behind me, smooth and laced with amusement.

"I wouldn't eat that if I were you."

I spun in midair to face the intruder, jumping what felt like three feet. But when I turned around, it was just me and the trees. Annoyed, I shook my head at myself as I bent over to pick up the berries I'd dropped. Only twelve hours alone in a strange place and I was already hallucinating?

"Of course, you can suit yourself."

I snapped back upright, scanning my surroundings and bracing myself for a fight. Something moved behind a nearby tree. Just as I turned to stare at it, a flicker of orange darted by and disappeared behind another tree closer to me. This thing was toying with me. Making a big show of being irritated, I crossed my arms, hiding my hands while I shifted them into claws, and tapped a foot.

"Who or *what*ever you are, you can show yourself, because I'm pretty much sick of this place and its games."

"Is that how you treat new acquaintances where you're from? Manners, manners."

This time, the voice was right behind me. I turned around slowly, refusing to appear afraid, chin tilted up in defiance. My eyes met . . . nothing. There wasn't anyone in front of me, except for, dropping my eyes, a large fox.

"You've got to be kidding me," I said to nobody in particular.

I blinked, rubbing my eyes, but when I opened them, the fox was still there—the apparent source of the voice.

The fox licked an inky-black paw, then looked at me, opened its mouth, and . . . words came out. "I'm afraid I'm not in on the joke."

"But you're . . . you're a fox," I stammered. "Do all animals talk here?"

He paced around me. I wasn't too clear on how big foxes were supposed to be, but he seemed bigger than normal— at least two feet tall at the shoulder. Judging by the size of the trees, "bigger than normal" was the real normal here. I shifted my hands back, eyeing him with suspicion.

"Of course not. That would be silly. Do all animals talk wherever you're from?" Everything that came from his mouth sounded just a little sarcastic. It would have gotten under my skin in normal circumstances. Right now, though, my brain was still stuck on the talking fox issue and lacked its regular ready supply of snarky comments.

"Um, none of them do, thanks very much."

He gave a cackling laugh, a weird mix of snorting, high-pitched yips, and barks. "I doubt that. I'm sure they do and you just don't listen."

*Whatever* was going on at this particular moment, and *however* bewildering it was, it wasn't getting me any closer to finding the White Woman, Logan, or that damn road. I side-stepped around the fox. "Well, it was very nice to meet you, Mr. Fox, but—"

He cut me off, moving in front of me. "Forgive me! I chastised you on your manners, and I haven't even properly introduced myself." To my astonishment, he dropped into a deep bow, with a flourish of his tail. "I am Reynard. It is a pleasure to make your acquaintance." He sat up again and flashed me a sharp-toothed smile. "And may I ask with whom am I speaking?"

"I . . . " I dragged it out, remembering Logan's warning about names and trying to buy time to think. "You can call me Jane." Talk about boring aliases. I needed to make a better one up for next time.

The answering yip of laughter bounced off the trees. "What I can *call* you is not the same thing as your name, but I understand. The forest is a dangerous place, and you look lost."

Sighing, I let my defenses down a little. After all, he seemed harmless, bordering on friendly. "I kind of am. Do you want to help your new friend out and give me some directions? I need to find the White Woman of the Forest."

Reynard cocked his head and I could practically hear the wheels turning behind those crafty amber eyes. "Looking for the White Woman, eh? That's not a popular request. Tell me, does she know you are seeking her?"

I shook my head, trying to look less desperate than I felt. "No, but, uh, a friend told me I need to find her."

"Mmm." He resumed licking his paw and cleaning his ear without a care in the world. "Why?"

"Honestly? I don't know. I don't know who she is, but if Lo—my friend told me to find her, that's what I should do. I trust him. I'm trying to help . . . another friend."

He stopped grooming and studied me again with that too-smart gaze. "I believe we might have a mutual friend." His ivory teeth flashed in an unnervingly sharp smile. "Due to that, and because I find this situation interesting, I'll help." He shook himself and stretched, then trotted out in front of me. "If you keep going in this direction"—he pointed with his nose—"you'll meet the White Woman."

I took a few tentative steps and glanced back, still not quite sure I could trust him. "She lives that way?"

More laughter. I rolled my eyes as he strolled behind me. "You'll run into her. Don't worry. Just remember, you owe me a favor now."

I turned to make a snotty retort, but he was gone. I *had* to learn how to do that, because apparently it was de rigueur here. I set out the way he'd pointed. Now that I had some directions, I was determined to get as far as I could in one day before stopping to sleep. I was feeling extra-motivated to meet this White Woman and hoped she could help me finally make some progress toward my actual goal of helping the kidnapped kids, and maybe reunite me with Logan in the process. Aside from that, I very much disliked the idea of sleeping alone in this forest.

The moon was high, my eyelids were drooping, and my legs felt like lead. I didn't want to stop. I knew if I did, I wouldn't be able to force myself into getting back up again.

I didn't know if it was the exhaustion, the darkness, or just sheer inexperience that I didn't see it coming, but I walked right out into an open clearing. Startled, I staggered back into the shelter of the trees and took stock of my surroundings. I wasn't at the edge of the woods—just a break in it. This must be the road that Rowan and Logan had been talking about. I paused for a moment, trying to decide if Reynard had meant for me to follow the road or to cross it. My dog-tired thoughts wandered circles around each other. Frustrated, I decided I was too tired to think straight. I'd cross the road and make camp (or rather, pass out in the first dry spot I found) on the other side. After a few hours of sleep, with a clearer mind, I could figure out what to do next.

Glancing around, I stepped out from the trees. The packed-dirt road was about twenty feet wide, with a deep ditch on either side. I crept into the ditch, which was almost shoulder high. Not seeing or hearing anyone on the road, I decided it was safe to cross. I'd run across in one sprint and make it to the other ditch before I stopped. I pulled myself out and darted onto the road, running as fast as my burning legs would carry me. Almost there . . . but then the horizon pitched sideways as I tripped on a rock and tumbled headfirst onto the wet ground.

After a lengthy moment where my mind caught up with my body, I propped myself up and did a mental inventory. Scraped and bleeding palms, a scratch on my jaw, a bruised knee. Not ideal, but nothing I couldn't handle. I rolled over to push myself up when I heard hoofbeats approaching in the distance. Panicking, I tried to stand up, but a sharp pain stabbed in my left ankle and I fell back over. Shit—I'd sprained it and it wouldn't hold any weight. I'd deal with that later. If I could just make it into the ditch, I should be safe. I rolled back onto my hands and knees and scrambled toward the ditch . . . so close . . .

But the hoofbeats were right there, and now there were voices, too. "Whoa!" one yelled. They stopped about ten feet from me. Grimacing, I looked up to see two men—elves, rather—on horses. They were both dressed in brown leather pants and heavy gray tunics belted at the waist, with a sheathed sword stuck in the belt. The overall impression was one of practical utility. These guys didn't carry swords around for show, and they weren't wearing heavy armor that would slow them down.

One dismounted in a single fluid motion and looked at me with a combination of interest and disdain writ large on his face. "What's this? How did you get out here?"

I forced myself to stand and face him, favoring my bad foot and trying hard to sound casual. "It's kind of a long story. I don't want to waste your time. I'll just, you know, be on my way . . . " As I turned, he materialized at my side with a viselike grip on my upper arm, laughing. Ugh. Elf speed. His partner was dismounting, too. This was not good.

The one gripping my arm started to drag me back toward the horses. "I think she escaped somehow," he said to the other, acting as though I couldn't hear him. "We need to get her back to the castle, like the others." I squirmed, trying to wriggle away. "Stop that," he barked at me as the other guard grabbed my free arm, which I'd been flailing around in an attempt to keep my balance. In the tussle, my sleeve was pushed up past the wrist, showing part of my Mark.

"Hey," he said, speaking over me as if I were cattle, "look at this. The others don't have these, right?"

He turned my arm over and pushed my sleeve all the way up to my elbow, showing the full length of my Mark. The first guard looked at it, interested. "No, I don't think so."

Taking advantage of their momentary confusion, I dipped into my already low energy reserves and shifted my hands into claws. While they'd been examining my arm, the first guard's grip had relaxed just enough to give me an out. In one swift motion, I pulled my arm back and then raked my claws across his back, shredding the tunic and making him cry out in surprise.

He spun around and snarled. "What *are* you?" The other guard was already behind me, pinning my arms to my side and lifting me up off the ground. I dug my claws into his thighs and twisted. The first guard approached, looking me up and down. I kicked at him with my good foot, trying to keep him at a distance.

"Whatever you are"—his sword hissed a metallic warning as he unsheathed it—"I don't think Her Highness will be too upset if we bring you in injured. Or even"—his teeth glinted white in the moonlight as he grinned at me without mirth—"dead."

The adrenaline of facing an actual life-or-death situation gave me the small energy boost I needed to extend my claws more. They sank several inches into the legs of the guard holding me up. As I twisted my hands, working deeper into the muscle, he screamed and finally dropped me. I cried aloud as all my weight was forced onto my injured foot, but managed to roll onto my hands and knees. I crawled away as fast as I could. *Think, Tania, there has to be a way out of this, come on . . .*

A hard kick to the stomach interrupted my desperate scramble to safety. The next blow tossed me onto my back. Gasping for air, I tried to keep moving, but I couldn't. The burst of adrenaline combined with exhaustion had left me shaky and weak, and the two kicks had left me unable to breathe. My body wouldn't obey my commands, no matter how dire the situation was.

The first guard was a silhouette against the full moon, his sword raised high. He changed his grip on the sword, and, without mercy or hesitation, drove it into my stomach. My vision dimmed and sparked. Somewhere that seemed very far away, I heard my screams and his answering laughter. Clinging to consciousness by my fingernails, I hoped that maybe, just maybe, there was still a way out of this, but no. Maybe not.

Maybe I should just give in to the soft, numb darkness that was surrounding me.

In that same distant place, the laughter was cut short with a bellowing roar and several thuds. A tiny part of me wondered what was going on, but really, I just wanted to rest. Things became quiet again. I was vaguely aware of something picking me up and cradling me, like a child. Huge yellow eyes with horizontal irises stared at me, but they were only just visible through the thick haze of pain and shock. As I was carried off into the woods, I finally, mercifully, lost consciousness.

# CHAPTER TEN

Staring out the car window, I pouted in the way only a sullen teenager can. The deafening silence had lasted the full fifteen minutes since we'd left the doctor's office. Finally, my mom broke it as we sat at a stoplight.

"Titania . . ." She reached out and brushed my shoulder. I twisted in my seat to jerk just out of her reach. Refusing to acknowledge her, I pretended I was alone and kept staring out the window. Cue her titanic sigh. "You know I don't like these doctor visits any more than you do."

I snorted. "Then why do you keep dragging me to them, Mom? This is the third specialist in three weeks. You know what they're going to say, because they keep saying it. No explanation. No solution. I'm just a fucking freak now, and that's that."

"Titania, *language*." She inhaled long and deep through her nose and exhaled, an indignant puff. "Obviously, nobody is happy about this . . . this turn of events. That's no excuse to act like a brat." Her voice softened, taking on a pleading note. "I'm just trying to help."

I went back to ignoring her, scowling at the street signs as I picked at a loose thread in the cuff of my sleeve. As if being a teenager with a social life in dire need of CPR wasn't bad enough. Being pulled against my will into this global event, or catastrophe, or *whatever*, made it worse. We'd been out of school for the last two weeks, since other students were having the same . . . issues as me.

The cherry on the shit sundae was that stress and hormones seemed to make the problem worse. You can't do much about hormones as a teenager. And stress kind of comes with the territory when you discover you have supernatural powers you can't quite control. Once it became clear that some students had glamoured their way into better grades, the district decided a temporary break was best for everyone. Schools all over the country were doing the same thing. Given that it was May, there was talk of just calling the rest of the school year a wash in the face of this mess.

Stewing in my moodiness, I watched the street crawl by. Mom gave up trying to talk to me, my foul temper transforming her frustration into anger. Instead of making conversation, she swore under her breath at drivers and the traffic lights. There was one particularly long verbal blue streak after a light turned *red* just as we approached the intersection we'd been waiting to cross for ten minutes.

"Well," I said, snotty, "I'm glad that it's not okay for *me* to use that kind of language when we're talking about my actual life, but you can cuss all you want about traffic."

She squeezed her eyes shut and pinched her nose. "Tania, now is not the time. We're both tired. It's been a long day, and this traffic is ridiculous. We can talk about it later."

"Of course we can talk about it when *you* want to talk

about it," I snapped. "We talk about *everything* when you want
to. We don't talk about how this is affecting me. We don't talk
about when you're going to accept that this is clearly not going
away. It's been weeks, Mom. I know it's not your idea of fun,
but when are you going to face facts and accept that this"—
I slammed my hand down on the dash, my voice so loud it
echoed inside the car—"is our new reality?"

She raised her voice to match mine. "That is enough. You
will *not* speak to me that way. I'm still your mother, no matter
what."

"You know what? You're right. That is enough. Have
fun sitting in traffic. I'm going to find another way home." I
slammed the door as hard as I could and stomped off. Her
muffled yells followed me. I'd pay for this later, but right now,
I didn't care. I was shaking with anger. Swallowing, I blinked
back tears. Refusing to be seen crying in public, I threw up my
hood and stuck my hands in my pockets. After a few blocks,
though, I ran out of steam, and my irate march turned into a
grumpy stroll.

Coming out of my blinding rage, I noticed that something
really was holding up traffic. Everyone was honking, and ob-
scenities peppered the air—Mom wasn't the only cranky one.
I heard yells coming from a few blocks ahead. I picked up my
pace again, curious and willing to indulge in any distraction.

The shouting grew in volume faster than I'd expected.
I couldn't tell if it was because I was getting closer, or if the
number of people yelling was increasing. Next came the crisp
crunch of something hitting glass, then the tell-tale tinkling
of a window shattering on the sidewalk. Maybe I *shouldn't* be
walking this way. Heart pounding, I turned into an alley, just
as a surge of people drew closer on the sidewalk. I ducked behind a dumpster, peeking out to see what was going on.

"They're going to take over!" screamed one woman.

"Nobody can explain why they're here or what's going on," snarled another voice, hysterical. "It's a sign of the end times. They're going to kill us all!"

A third person chimed in with something about "the fucking freaks." A wet thud came from the crowd as someone threw a boy, who couldn't have been any older than eighteen, to the ground. One of his eyes was already swollen and purple. His arms were raised above his head, a futile shield in the face of the blows raining down.

"You're one of them!"

"Tell us what you people are going to do!"

He replied in shuddering gasps, sobbing so hard it was hard to understand him. Bloody teeth flashed around his words. "I don't know anything. There is no plan, please, I have a mom looking for me, please let me go . . . " The mob circled him and there were more thuds, coupled with scared-animal whimpers.

I crouched behind the dumpster, hands clamped over my mouth to keep from screaming, eyes squeezed shut. I tried to reason with whatever external force might be listening. *Please don't let them find me, I'll never yell at my mom again, I'll get straight As in school, I'll go to a good college, just like she wants, please, please don't let them find me . . .*

Jerked out of that nightmare of a memory, I found myself in darkness. Somewhere in the back of my brain, I dimly recalled being run through with a sword. Was this what it was like to be dead? Trying to move, I found I couldn't: thick rope bound my arms and ankles to a roughly hewn table that I could only just see if I twisted my head. I screamed, but a wad of cloth stuffed in my mouth choked it out.

Out of the pitch, a woman emerged. White hair, knotted high on her head, stood out against the inky backdrop. Yellow eyes, predatory and inhuman, glinted against creased, leathery skin. A bright crimson kerchief covered most of her face, completing the "you're about to get murdered real good" vibe.

She set down a basket of twigs and straw with a dull thud. Struggling against the bonds, I realized with horror that I was numb all over. I should have bruised or cut myself with how hard I was kicking and fighting, but I couldn't feel anything—not even the sword wound. The woman untied the kerchief for a moment, revealing a large hooked nose and a mouth like a straight gash in her face. She inspected me, and I could swear I saw a sparkle of pity in her eyes.

"I am sorry," she said, gazing down at me, "but for you to survive and be stronger, it must be done."

Ignoring my strangled yells, she retied the kerchief over her face, then bent over to retrieve a sickle-shaped knife from the basket. She pulled up my ragged shirt, still soaked in blood, and studied my stomach. Eyes wide with panic, I tried to talk around the gag again, but the only thing that came out was "*mmph plmf ungh.*" She didn't even look at my face. With a swipe of the blade, precise and fast, she split open my stomach and dug her hand in deep. I screamed again, even as I realized I couldn't feel any pain—just the horrifying, unsettling sensation of someone's hand inside my abdomen. It was like being at the dentist: your mouth is numb, but you can still tell someone is poking around in there. She pulled her hand out, and viscera plopped onto the ground beside me. With her other hand—the one that had been holding the knife—she grabbed a handful of branches and forced them into my stomach cavity. She repeated the same motions, over and over again. Guts out, twigs in. I kept screaming, or trying to. I couldn't breathe. Shock set in, narrowing my vision into pinpricks. My head lolled to the side, and I drifted back into unconsciousness.

I was somewhere else again, standing outside a navy-blue building, underneath a low, slate-gray sky, wailing in grief and terror. I felt like I was inside myself, yet observing the scene unfold like a movie. A cold, detached voice in my head asked me what was going on. This wasn't a memory.

I didn't have time to keep wondering. The building exploded with solar-flare force and knocked me ass-over-tea-kettle to the dewy grass. Dampness crept through my clothes to cover my back, and I opened my eyes—screaming at the top of my lungs, arms and legs thrashing in panic.

# CHAPTER ELEVEN

was definitely in a bed, on a straw mattress by the feel of it, buried underneath a pile of hand-quilted blankets in folksy colors and patterns. Panting from terror and confusion, I swung my feet around to the side of the bed. I didn't see a weapon nearby, but maybe I could improvise.

"I wouldn't stand just yet if I were you. You've been through a lot."

I almost jumped out of my skin. Looking around, I appeared to be in a quaint one-room cottage, complete with rocking chair and roaring fire. The chair creaked loudly as a woman stood up and faced me. Her white hair glowed, tinted gold by the fire, and fell around her shoulders like a crystal waterfall, framing her porcelain face. It was held back by a yellow strip of fabric, and her dress was a matching golden color, with similar folksy patterns as the quilts. Eight-pointed stars and roses intertwined around its hem, and she'd tied a white apron over it. Her frame was slight but muscular. She looked like a

Russian Folktale Barbie—except for the inhuman, predatory eyes I'd seen in my dream. They glinted at me and I scrambled back onto the bed, bumping into the wall.

"Ah. You remember. I rather hoped you wouldn't, it's not a pleasant thing. But"—she shrugged—"what must be done must be done."

"Seriously, lady?" My throat was tight with fear, my voice squeaky. "You cut me open!"

She looked me over again, her face expressionless. "Look at your wound."

This had to be a trick. I stayed still and maintained eye contact, waiting for her to attack me. She just stared back, unblinking. In an effort to escape her unnerving gaze, I looked at my stomach. I lifted the edge of my shirt and almost dropped it in surprise. There wasn't a wound. There weren't even any stitches. It was like it had never happened. The only difference was a thin spun-silver line that reached from one hipbone to the other.

I smoothed my shirt over my stomach and eyed her, satisfied she wasn't going to kill me. But I was still suspicious. Nice people didn't get things done by cutting others open and pulling out their insides, after all. Looking her up and down, I leaned back against the rough cabin wall and crossed my arms. "Who are you?"

"You already know who I am. I'm the White Woman of the Forest. Your friend told you to find me, did he not?"

I blinked. "How do you know that?"

She took a few steps toward me. I scooted back a fraction of an inch, not wanting her any closer than necessary, but also not wanting to appear weak or scared. The woman paused for a moment, a foot or two away, giving me that strange emotionless look again. Then she closed the gap between us and brushed a finger against my forehead. "He marked you. It's a clear warning not to harm you. I recognize his touch."

So Logan had sent me to a shapeshifting witch that lived in the woods and cut people open. I'd have to remember to thank him for that. I touched my forehead, remembering how Logan had kissed it before running off. It *had* been an unusually affectionate gesture, but I'd assumed it was the result of the dire situation. I guess there'd been another, more practical reason.

"Why would you help him—or me?"

"I owe him a favor. I assume helping you is part of that, although healing and protection work is rather outside of that bargain."

I shuddered at the memory of being tied to the table. "You have a funny way of healing people, lady."

She flashed a grin at me, one full of bright white teeth, rather sharper than normal. "Sometimes you have to take things apart before they will go back together properly."

Shifting on the bed, I broke the awkward pause. "Well. Thanks. I guess. So, is 'White Woman' a name or a title or what?"

Turning away, she stoked the fire. "It is not my name or a proper title, but you wouldn't know my name, anyway. I have been called She of the Iron Nose and the Lady of the Wilderness, but I do not think you'll recognize those, either. For the most part, your people don't talk much about me anymore." She flashed that toothy smirk again over her shoulder. "That suits me quite well. At any rate, you may call me Birke."

Reynard's remark about names echoed in my head. Smoothing her apron, Birke perched at the end of the bed and crossed her legs at the ankles. The very picture of poise. "You have some power in you. May I see it?"

"Uh," I said, taken aback by the abruptness of the request.

"Sure. Do you want to see anything in specific?" She shook her head, her eyes lingering on my face. I shrugged. Tapping into my energy, I was surprised to find it ready and waiting, so I flashed through a series of demonstrations: my old standby glamour of "plenty of makeup and well-done hair," followed in quick succession by a "don't see me" glamour and my weaponized claws.

She made a small noise of appraisal. "Is there anything else? Do you have any particular affinities?"

I shook my head, then corrected myself. "Maybe. That was most of the stuff I had to do to get by back home. It's harder to do there than it is here, and I just didn't ever experiment much, I guess. But sometimes I dream things and then they happen."

She nodded. "Clairvoyant dreams, you mean?"

I scrunched my nose. "That's always seemed like a pretentious word to me, but I guess that's what it is."

Birke settled onto the bed, which groaned in reluctance at having two people on it. Leaning one shoulder against the wall and crossing her arms, she studied me. "And what is your purpose for being here? You are certainly not of this world."

I snorted. "No, definitely not. We don't have snotty talking foxes where I'm from, for one thing."

For the first time, she laughed, a bright peal reminiscent of tiny bells. "Reynard? He's an acquired taste, but I would not speak ill of him if I were you. He alerted my folk that you were in my woods looking for me. Without him, they may not have found you and brought you to me in time."

"Well, snarky foxes aside, I came here with Logan because children are going missing back home, and someone here is taking them."

"And by 'someone,' you mean the ruler of these lands, yes?"

"Yeah, her. Logan's sister, Gwyneira."

Uncrossing her arms, she stood up and rearranged her skirt and apron to lie flat again. "I see why he sent you to me. Someone taking children in groups, unprovoked, is *quite* in my jurisdiction." Frowning, she stared at a point on the wall, thinking what looked like unpleasant thoughts. "Especially without consulting me first."

Her attention snapped back to me. "Stand up," she ordered, waving a hand. "I want to look at you."

I pushed the blankets to the side and stood up. Now that the adrenaline rush had passed, I was a little weak and woozy, but that was it. I didn't even feel like I'd taken a real beating. I knew what that felt like, and I couldn't feel any aches or bruises anywhere. More than anything else, it felt like I was coming off a minor cold.

Starting at my left, Birke circled all the way around me, looking me up and down and murmuring under her breath. Then she walked the opposite direction and motioned for me to turn so she could see my back. I was completely mystified, but Logan must have sent me here for a reason.

"All right, you may sit." I sat back down and pulled the blankets around me, warming back up. "You have potential. I will help with your quest if"—she held up a warning finger—"you're willing to be trained."

"Uh, trained how?"

"I will give you time to heal. In the meantime, we will work on that potential of yours. If you want to have any hope of bringing those orphans back home, you'll need to practice. And of course, once you're feeling better, you'll help out around here. I owe Logan, but I don't owe him *that* much. I cannot abide idleness."

I thought back to Logan's warning about not taking gifts. "Will this . . . arrangement . . . create any kind of lasting bond between us? Will I be in *your* debt once we're done?"

She laughed again, but this time it wasn't a pretty tinkling of bells. It was a much darker laugh, showing her *definitely* pointier than normal teeth. "I saved your life and put you under my protection. I effectively initiated you to be one of Mine. There's already a lasting bond between us, whether you like it or not."

"But . . . but that's not fair," I spluttered. "I never agreed to that!"

"Would you rather be bleeding out from a stomach wound, with the forest's predators starting their meal before you are done dying? Or in the castle, the guards torturing you for fun?"

"Uh . . ."

She inclined her head in a half nod. "Precisely. Besides, it's not so bad being one of Mine. I might ask you to do things on occasion, but you're under my protection as well, which is formidable." I had no doubt of *that*, at least. Her eyes shone in the firelight like a cat's, green-brown and iridescent, and her teeth gleamed.

"Well." I swallowed hard. "Then I guess we have an agreement. You'll train me, I'll save the kids. So when do we start?"

What felt like an eternity later, I flopped back on the bed, drenched in sweat and panting. We'd done round after round of glamours of every type and shifting every part of my body. The glamouring wasn't so bad, but the shifting had really done me in.

I was exhausted, and it looked like twilight had well and truly turned into night. The still-full moon sent blue light streaming through the windows, where it met the fire's flickering orange light.

"We're done for now," I gasped between pants, "right?"

She gave me an amused look from where she sat in the rocking chair. "Yes. I would offer you dinner, but I imagine you aren't hungry."

Surprised, I found she was right. Even though I was bone tired, my stomach wasn't growling at all. "Why not?"

"It's a side effect of the initiation. Your appetite will return tomorrow, don't worry. You'll also be feeling much better, which means a full day of training. We'll start by exploring your potential."

I propped myself up on my elbows. "That sounds thrilling. I can't wait," I replied, trying and mostly failing to keep the sarcasm out of my voice.

Birke lifted an eyebrow. "You *should* be excited. I would tell you this is a once in a lifetime opportunity, but really, it would be more like once in ten or twenty lifetimes."

"Yeah. I'm sorry." I sighed. "I *do* appreciate your help. With Logan gone, I'm pretty much a lost babe in the woods." I laughed at the phrase, then my face dropped as I stared into the fire, thinking. "I hope he's okay."

"He's alive," she replied. "I am certain of that."

I perked back up. "What? How do you know?"

She motioned at my forehead again. "If he were dead, his mark on you would have faded. It's still there. He's alive."

I let out a huge breath. "Oh man. I'm so glad he's okay."

Her eyebrows drew together, and she looked away. "I don't know if 'okay' is the word I would use. The forest wights are whispering—"

I interrupted. "The what?"

"The wights. The spirits of the forest, the trees, the land. They say he wasn't captured by the Hunt. If that is true, then he was likely captured by someone else. Otherwise, he would have been able to track you down. This close to the castle, chances are his sister's men found him and brought him in. If that's so, it's only a matter of time before she has him executed."

"You *really* think she'd have him executed?" From everything I'd heard, she wasn't one to pull punches. But there's a difference between being power hungry and being ruthless enough to kill your own brother. Some part of me was pleading with reality, hoping it would bend to my will.

She kept staring into the fire. "I know she would. And according to the laws of the land, she has every right to. Even if the circumstances around it are wrong, he *was* banished. The penalty of trespassing after being outlawed is death. There are few who would protest."

The room splintered into a mosaic of light and shadow as tears welled in my eyes. No *wonder* he'd been so adamant about not returning. I buried my face in my hands, fighting back the onslaught of tears. "I got him into this mess. This is my fault. He only came to help me."

The chair squeaked as she stood and walked across the room to stand at the door. "This will put us on a shorter timeline. If you want to save your friend, you have at most a week to prepare."

I lifted my head, wallowing in despair. "What if that's not enough time?"

Her hand on the door, she rested those eerie eyes on me again, gauging my reaction or maybe just thinking. "Then you keep training and become stronger, but let your friend die."

I shook my head. "That's not an option."

She shrugged as she turned to walk out the door. "Then I suggest you get a good night's rest."

"Hey, wait! Where are you going?"

She looked over her shoulder and grinned. This time, it wasn't just a sharp-toothed smile—it was a predatory snarl.

That same instinct that urged me to run when I was out-matched in a fight warned me not to push it.

"Hunting."

With that, she walked out, the door softly closing behind her. Sighing, I lay down and rolled onto my side to stare at the wall until I fell asleep.

I was greeted in the morning to the sound of sizzling and a mouthwatering smell hanging in the air. Sitting up, I rubbed the sleep from my eyes. My hostess was crouched by the fire and turning what looked like a whole pig leg on a spit, fat dripping in the flames. Finally, some real food—no more bruised apples. Swinging my legs around the bed, I stood up to stretch.

Birke took her attention off the fire for a moment. "Good morning."

I yawned and moved closer, eager for some breakfast. "That smells delicious."

"Not so fast. There's wood to chop out back." I protested, but she silenced me with a wave of her hand and a stern look. "Consider it part of our bargain. Especially now that we're on an accelerated timeline."

Grumbling under my breath, I found my boots at the foot of the bed. I was still in the clothes I'd been wearing when the guards had attacked me. I'd need to change at some point—my shirt was covered in dried blood and had a sizable hole in it. That could wait, though. A large pile of firewood, nearly as tall as me, was waiting patiently to be chopped outside.

"Seriously?" I whined, my stomach chiming in with a rumble. If Birke could hear me inside, she didn't acknowledge me. Better to get it over with fast instead of trying to talk my way out of it.

Turns out, chopping wood was a lot harder than it looked, but I finally got the hang of it after a few false starts. I stacked the split wood against the side of the cabin, where it was somewhat sheltered from the elements. Finally, time for some real food.

Birke appeared to have already eaten and motioned for me to sit in the rocking chair. She handed me a plate with a heaping slab of meat on it. As I devoured the ham—which was delicious, despite being a little overcooked—she went outside to clean off the spit in the snow.

She returned just as I swallowed the last of my food. Now that I wasn't starving, I needed to fix the other pressing issue at hand before it became any more dire. "Do you have a shower or something?" She looked at me, uncomprehending. I sighed. "Look. I stink. I need to wash, and I need to get into some of my cleaner clothes."

"Ah. Yes. My folk grabbed your backpack." She gestured to the head of my bed, where my backpack was resting. "We're on a tight schedule and don't have time for you to bathe. My suggestion is to clean off as best as possible in the snow outside and have a full bath later."

"A sponge bath with snow?" I blanched, shaking my head for emphasis. "But . . . it's cold!"

She cocked her head, a quizzical expression on her face. "Is snow warm where you come from?"

"No, but . . ." I waved a hand at the window. "I'll freeze!"

Birke shrugged, turning away. "It won't kill you. It's either that or heat water over the fire and pour it into a bathing basin. And we need to get started with your training. Do a snow bath or wait until tomorrow, the decision is yours. But be quick about deciding." She was looking at shelves on the far wall, picking up this item and that, unconcerned with my choice.

I hesitated. You could probably smell me ten feet away,

and I had that all-over grimy feeling. I didn't want to put on clean clothes when I was this dirty, but I was tired of wearing filthy ones.

"Fine," I grumbled and stomped outside. I looked around and chose a large tree so I'd feel a little less exposed. I hesitated as I took off my jacket, very much not looking forward to this. I decided a rip-the-Band-Aid-off approach would be best and kicked off my shoes and jeans in quick succession, then removed my shirt as fast as I could.

The cold made me gasp. Goosebumps popping up all over my body and shivering already, I bent down to grab handfuls of fresh snow and scrubbed myself. It wasn't a replacement for a real bath, but given that the snow was turning a disgusting shade of gray-brown, it was definitely an improvement.

As I was wrapping up, I realized I'd omitted a big part of my plan: I didn't have a towel, and I didn't want to put back on my dirty clothes. Swearing a blue streak to match my frosty lips, I burst into the cabin, trying to maintain my modesty despite juggling a pile of clothes and my boots. Birke was still standing at the shelves. She gestured toward the fireplace. "You can warm up by the fire, if you wish."

Teeth chattering, I dragged my backpack over to the fire and crouched behind it. Birke didn't seem bothered by my entire lack of clothing, but I've never been one to let it all hang out—and I was *not* about to start here in fairy land with a shapeshifting forest witch. The fire dried me off as I rubbed warmth back into my arms and legs, then pulled on clean clothes from my backpack. I stood up, feeling much better, although still not exactly squeaky clean.

I sighed. "Okay. Where do we start?"

Birke turned to face me. "Here," she said, handing me a flat piece of slate with two angular shapes drawn on it.

"What's this?" I turned it over, as if that would give me

a clue how I was supposed to use it. Flipping the stone back over, I rubbed one of the symbols. It came off on my finger. Nothing special here, just a plain old piece of rock, used as a makeshift chalkboard.

Birke pointed at the symbol that looked like a three-pointed trident. "These are called runes. They're useful for certain types of magic. I want to teach you one for defensive purposes and one for offensive purposes."

I tried not to sound skeptical. "Magic? Like potions and waving wands?"

She shook her head. "No. The magic uses the same source as your glamours. It's your energy, shaped and used for something that others can see." She sat down in the rocking chair and started rocking, her inscrutable face watching mine for a reaction. "To be honest, I'm not sure you'll be able to do it. I might be wrong about your potential. But since you don't seem to have a particular affinity, I think free-form work might be a good place to start."

I turned the slate over in my hands again, nervous about living up to her expectations and trying to stall. "Is it a bad thing to not have an affinity?"

"Mmm. There are pros and cons either way. You don't have any natural boundaries to contain your energy. That makes you more flexible. You can bend your energy to do whatever you have enough willpower to do. Someone who is bound to a certain element or landscape can't throw runes, for example. But not having a built-in container, so to speak, can make it more difficult and draining to use that energy. You have to create the container each time you do something new. You're not just drawing water from the well, but also creating the bucket to carry it in. Do you understand?"

I mulled it over, staring at the symbols. "It makes sense, I guess. But what does 'throwing runes' mean? Am I supposed to, like, throw this?" I motioned with the hand holding the rock.

"No, no. I just used the rock to show you what they look like. We will start with Algiz; it is less . . . aggressive." She pointed to the trident symbol. "Look at it and focus. Try to fill that shape with your energy."

I scrunched up my face, staring at the symbol. What she said didn't make any sense. Sensing my frustration, she elaborated a little. "You can gesture with your other hand to 'throw' the energy, if it will help you focus. That's why it's called 'throwing runes.'"

Closing my eyes, I dove into my inner well of energy, surprised to find it so full after the trauma of the last few days. I acted like I was going to do a glamour, but instead of thinking about what face I wanted to have, I focused on the shape of the rune. I could feel the energy pooling in my left hand, where I was trying to direct it. Squinting in concentration, I made a throwing motion, trying to force the energy out and away from me.

Opening my eyes the rest of the way, I gasped. Hanging in the air a few feet in front of me was the symbol, shimmering blue-green, as though it were made of stained glass. When I gasped, I lost my concentration and the symbol faded, dissipating like a puff of smoke in a sudden breeze.

Birke clapped. "That's very good for a first try! Well done."

I looked at my hands and then her, proud and mystified all at once. How had I never thought to try anything like that in my years of living as a Marked? If I could do that, what else could I do that I hadn't even imagined? Good questions, but I settled on a more pertinent one for now. "What does it do?"

"Let's go outside for a demonstration, shall we?"

I followed her out the door, grabbing my jacket. It might

be dirty and have a sword hole, but it was still the only outerwear I had.

She gestured for me to walk away from her. I walked about ten feet and looked at her for confirmation.

"A bit farther," she said, waving her hand. I backed up until I was closer to twenty feet away. "Now, run at me as if you were going to attack me."

I didn't bother asking why. I dug in my feet, making sure I'd have a decent start in the slippery snow, and kicked off, running at her as fast as I could. Birke stood still as a statue, watching me rush at her headlong, with no signs of moving. I had to fight the urge to veer away. Whatever she was planning, I had no intention of rolling around in the snow and mud to prove her point.

At any rate, I didn't get a chance to correct my course. Once I was six or seven feet away, she made a quick gesture with her hand—the same one I'd made in the cabin, but far more smooth and practiced. In an instant, the trident symbol hung in the air between us, and I ran face-first into it with a thud.

Bouncing back, I landed in the muddy snow. It felt somewhere between a brick wall and a trampoline. Not as much give as the former, but not enough resistance to injure me, either. Standing back up and brushing myself off, I poked it with my finger. I circled Birke, wondering if the shield only faced one way. The symbol—and its accompanying slightly squishy invisible wall—followed me as I paced around her.

Once my curiosity was satisfied, she dropped her hand and the symbol disappeared, lingering far longer than mine had in the process. "So," I said, musing aloud with my arms crossed and head tilted with intrigue, "it makes a force field around you?"

Birke mimicked my expression. "I don't know what you

mean by 'force field.' It creates a shield, which is excellent for defense. Use it in the right circumstances and you'll have enough time to get away or prepare a counterattack. Assuming, of course, that you can maintain it long enough. Which is why," she said as she walked back to the door, shaking the lingering snow off her skirt, "we're now going to practice your endurance."

We drilled Algiz for hours. We stopped for lunch, which consisted of another spit-roasted hunk of meat. If I hadn't already figured out she was a carnivore, the 100-percent-meat menu would have convinced me.

After a quick break to let the food settle, she gestured for me to go outside again. She followed me out, the door shutting behind her with a click. She put her hands on her hips. "Let's see how you fare in a real-world situation."

"Are you going to run at me now or something?"

No response.

When I looked behind me, she wasn't there. The small clearing outside her cabin had gone still and silent. My heartbeat sped up, loud in my ears, and my palms started to sweat. I took a few steps forward, hoping she'd pop up and tell me this was a joke, even though I knew she wasn't the practical-joke type. Or maybe she was just testing my reflexes. Several yards away, behind me, I heard a snort. I jumped, spinning to face the noise and digging my feet into the ground, already reaching for that wellspring of energy.

From behind a tree on the other end of the clearing, something stepped out. It was easily the strangest and most terrifying creature I'd seen since I arrived—or, you know, pretty much ever. Covered in shaggy, thick brown fur dappled with gray, it stood on two feet like a ten-foot-tall ape from Stephen King's nightmares. Arms as thick around as my waist hung from boulder-wide shoulders. It had a face like someone had taken your standard mountain goat, pushed the snout back into the skull, and gifted it with fierce yellow teeth that stuck out in a snarled mess. Spiraling horns added another two feet to its height, and huge golden eyes with horizontal irises and a surprising amount of intelligence behind them met mine. It snorted again, then hunched over and started to barrel right at me.

There was nowhere to hide unless I ran back inside the cottage, which would probably miss the point of this whole terrifying exercise. I might not be able to make it to the cabin in time, anyway. I scrabbled harder at my energy, pooling it in my hand while picturing the rune. As the creature drew closer, I threw out the energy and focused like my life depended on it. At the same time, I squeezed my eyes shut and crouched close to the ground. My hope was that if it didn't work, I'd be able to roll away. Maybe I'd only lose one limb in the process instead of all four.

A few seconds later, I wasn't missing *any* limbs, as far as I could tell. Scared of what I'd see, I peeked through one eye, then both of them. The creature was standing a safe distance away, on the other side of my very own radiant Algiz.

"Whoa," I whispered as the beast placed a bear-like paw the size of a frying pan on the shield and pushed a bit. When it didn't give in, the creature grunted and turned away.

Ringing laughter echoed in the otherwise silent woods as Birke stepped out from behind a pine tree. "Well done, Tania! I knew you had it in you." She grinned at me, then walked up to the creature and put a hand on its arm. Assuming that meant I'd passed the test, I relaxed and dropped my shield.

"Are you going to introduce me to your . . . er . . . friend here?" I gestured at it.

"Actually, you two have already met," she said, looking from me to the creature. "You aren't likely to remember it, though, given that you were bleeding from a mortal wound at the time. He's one of my folk who saved you from the guards."

"Oh," I said, taken aback. I guess Ms. Entrail Remover herself should have tipped me off, but I'd thought the good guys would look . . . well, nicer than this brown abominable-snowman knockoff. I stared up at him, maintaining eye contact as best I could given the height difference and the fact that, quite frankly, he still made me want to pee my pants a little bit.

"I appreciate the effort. Thank you for saving me," I said with a small bow. He grunted and thumped me on the shoulder, in a show of affection that knocked me off balance in the process and might have given me a minor case of whiplash.

Birke laughed again, clapping with glee. "He likes you! He doesn't take to many. You should consider yourself special."

I was currently in the Brothers' Grimm worst nightmare. I'd had my guts ripped out and replaced with twigs without my permission in some bizarre ritual. And now a creature that looked like he could eat velociraptors for breakfast had taken a liking to me.

"Oh, I do," I muttered. I looked back up into his yellow eyes. "Not that I don't appreciate your help"—I glanced at Birke for confirmation—"but don't we have more training to do?"

"There is always more training to do," she replied before facing the beast again, who leaned down to be on her eye level. "Thank you for your help today, and your continued loyal service." She scratched him behind one ear, like a loving dog owner, and kissed him on the tip of his snout. "We won't need your help again for the next day or so." He grunted, looked at me, and grunted again with a slight tilt of his head. I took that to be a good-bye and tried to mimic his head tilt in response. As he trundled off into the woods, Birke watched him go, then turned back to me.

"Let's go inside and learn your next rune," she said, gesturing to the door.

I groaned. She shot me an unamused look, and I back-pedaled. "Okay, okay, great, I can't wait," I said, holding up my hands in the universal gesture of surrender.

The next rune, Thurisaz, looked like a line with a pointy bump in the middle of it. Where Algiz was primarily useful for defense and protection, Thurisaz could be wielded like a ninja's throwing star. I kept that comparison to myself rather than try and explain it to her, but it held true all the same.

Birke taught me how to make a 3D energy rendering of the thorn-like symbol with the point facing out, then throw it at an attacker. It'd harm them mentally, physically, or both, depending on your intentions, power, and ability to focus. After that, she showed me how to create a ring of Thurisaz around myself, with the points facing out, in defense. It'd stop attackers in their tracks, while shredding an energetic or magical attack and marking it "return to sender." I'd be safe, and they'd get hit with their own energy *plus* the whomp of Thurisaz.

A few hours later, it was dinnertime and I was, once again, exhausted. We'd been drilling on the runes for most of the day, alternating between the two. I was getting much better at throwing them, but I needed a break and was grateful to have it, even if it was only to eat. Sitting on the floor, I tore into yet another roasted hunk of meat, this time goat. Birke rocked in her chair and stared into the fire, lost in thought.

"So," I said as I finished chewing and went in for another bite, "how'd you wind up the White Woman of the Forest? Is that a title that gets passed down?"

She blinked, her eyes refocusing on the room around us, and turned her tawny gaze on me. "Hmm? No. There is only one, and it has always been me. There is no story to be had there." She returned her gaze to the fire. "But there is another story that I think you should hear."

I scooted back to lean against the wall to make myself a little more comfortable and gave her my full attention.

# CHAPTER TWELVE

O nce upon a time, a long time ago, there lived a princess, in this very kingdom.

She wasn't a kind princess. Keeping the royal bloodlines pure was of paramount concern, you see, so inbreeding had taken quite the toll on the mental capacities of her father, the king. Her mother was well meaning, but we all know how much that accomplishes when it comes to good parenting. The king and queen cherished their daughter, and she grew up never wanting for anything. She was always assured she was correct in all matters, and was generally spoiled beyond the point of no return.

It was hard to blame the child. After all, what could she do about it? The king's advisors hoped she would grow out of it, as children sometimes do. Instead, she grew up into a terror. She lacked empathy or compassion. She savored the power she had over people and their fate. When she insisted on sitting in at court, it was a disaster. Her decisions lacked in both reason and mercy. She often pardoned criminals—whether their crime was violent or mundane, it mattered not. More often, she demanded the citizen be punished horribly, even if their trespass was minor. In fact, she was quite fond of amputations, and regularly insisted on supervising.

The wights knew that the princess's coronation would be a disastrous day for the land indeed. They convened to discuss their potential courses of action. The alfar wanted to wait and see how events progressed. The svartalfar were unconcerned, since what happened on the surface had little impact on them in their cave dwellings. The forest wights feared that she might set her hungry sights on their home and want to destroy the forest. Their concerns were valid. During at least one tantrum, she had expressed the opinion that the forest should be cut down for timber rather than stay a "boring, filthy waste of land" where "outcasts and witches" lived.

Those of us who had the power to take action—and had at least a passing fondness for the people of the kingdom—knew that something must be done. Given how I could easily disguise myself, I was to infiltrate the castle as an old maid and assess how bad the situation truly was.

Between the king's less than stellar intellect and my magic, I was inside the castle in very little time. I spent the first few days on my best behavior, and then I started my investigation.

I asked a young scullery maid, "What do you think of the princess?"

She immediately dropped her eyes and said, "Beg your pardon, but we mustn't talk of such things. It isn't polite."

The sharp tang of fear hung heavy in the air. The poor girl was trembling at the mere thought of my pressing her further. Instead, I dropped the subject and offered to take over the rest of her cleaning for the day. She fled the room and avoided me for the rest of that day and the next.

*I asked a head cook in the kitchen, "What do you think of the princess?"*

*He was also afraid. But mixed with the scent of fear was a burning rage. He looked around to see if anyone else was within earshot. Satisfied that we were alone, he spat over his shoulder.*

*"She's mad," he said angrily. "And not in the simple way her father is. In the worst way, in the cruel way. A few years ago, for no reason we could figure out, the princess decided that the cook appointed to prepare her meals was trying to poison her. She hired a taster and insisted on taking her meals privately, so the cook wouldn't know—to catch him red-handed, y'see. Of course, gossip gets around the castle. He knew he was in trouble. But he also knew that if he left, it would be an admission of guilt. The princess would have her father's guard hunt him down."*

*He took a breath. "She grew tired of the taster not detecting any poison. She decided that the taster and the cook must be working together, in a plot to usurp her kingdom. She had them both hanged in the town square, in front of their families. Then she exiled them, in case they harbored such treachery as well."*

*He looked me in the eye—something which is not easy for most mortals to do. "If they heard me discussing such things, they'd hang me for treason and punish my family. I trust you won't repeat it."*

*I found one last person to question, a handmaid who had previously worked in the princess's quarters. She was around the age I appeared to be—that is to say, quite elderly. I asked her, "What do you think of the princess?"*

*She reacted with neither terror nor anger, but sad acceptance. "You know how it is, when you get to be our age. You see some good, kind rulers. I wasn't old enough to work in the castle then, but I heard about her great-grandfather. He was one of them." She paused, a distant look in her eye, then continued, "The princess is neither good nor kind. She will use her cunning to* bring the kingdom to its knees, if she thinks it will get her what she wants. We must weather it the best we can, and if we are lucky, she shouldn't rule too long." She gave me a wan smile, patted me on the shoulder, and toddled off to finish her work.

Given the answers I received, I knew something must be done. The princess was not fit to rule. If the impulse struck her, she would have no problem destroying my own beloved forest, which I had sworn to protect. I decided to return to the forest and call a council meeting. Surely, the alfar and svartalfar would see reason in light of the stories I had collected.

I overheard a whispered conversation in the hall between two maids—handmaids to the king, in fact. I blended into my surroundings and willed them to talk a little louder. They complied.

"His condition hasn't improved?"

"No. If anything, it's worse. The court physician doesn't know what's wrong. But he does know that if the king's condition doesn't improve, his soul will leave us within a day. Maybe less."

That changed things. With the king dead, the princess would ascend the throne, with terrible results. I had to act fast. In an ideal situation, I would have returned to the forest and updated my kin. Then we would have decided on an appropriate course of action together. However, in this case, I feared there wasn't enough time. The others would regard an assassination, though well within my powers, as crossing the line. And as much as I loathed politics, I had only just gotten back on the good side of the alfar after several centuries.

My feet moving as fast as my thoughts, I ducked into the first room I found. For privacy, I cast a quick glamour on the door so it would appear to be a wall to everyone who passed it.

What was the answer? I couldn't kill her, but I couldn't let her rule, either. If I took her into my custody and held her captive in the forest, her mother would send all the castle soldiers after me. My forest, the home I'd sworn to protect, would become a battleground.

No. I simply needed to remove her from the game for the time being. Given more time, I could return to the forest and share my findings.

I stopped my pacing for a moment and looked around the room. By sheer force of fate, I found myself in the princess's dressing chambers. An almost finished gown hung on one wall, with a headdress and gloves on a table next to it. As I stared at the dress, wondering why one would wear such a garish, gaudy thing, an idea came to me.

I snatched the unfinished gloves from the table and grabbed a few other items from around the room. Lifting the glamour, I strode down the hall, casting a working on the items in my hands. It was a complex one, and powerful, too, but for someone of my age and experience, it wasn't difficult. I asked the passing servants where the princess was.

I found her outside her father's chambers, yelling at one of the servants for bringing soup that was too hot. I approached and curtsied as low as I could.

"Beg your pardon, Your Highness, but I have some final fittings to do and was wondering if you had a moment to spare . . ."

She whirled to face me and gave me a cold once-over. The berated servant seized the opportunity to scuttle off, glancing back as he escaped.

"How dare you interrupt me and make demands on my time? Now? What's your name, you filthy old hag? I'll make sure you starve for lack of work."

If I hadn't already decided against an assassination, I would have ripped her throat out then and there for daring to speak to me in such a manner. Instead, I bit back my rage and bowed again, murmuring, "I mean no harm . . . You want to be at your best for the upcoming autumn ball, but I'm sure you will look fine without the gloves. Nobody will fault you for any flaws in your attire, with your father in such a state . . ."

"Please," she huffed, "what would you know about fashion? I cannot attend a ball in incomplete regalia, no matter the circumstances. Here, give me that!"

She grabbed the gloves from me, almost tearing them in the process. She stuffed her hands in one and tugged it on. An ear-piercing shriek echoed down the hallway.

"What. Is. This?" she screeched with each yank of the offending glove, trying to remove it as hastily as she had put it on. She finally unsheathed her hand and waved it in my face. Lodged in one fingertip was a silver sewing needle.

"I will have you hanged for this, crone! How could you be so stupid?"

She clearly expected me to pull the affronting needle out. Instead, I took a step back and studied her, my face expressionless. This, of course, only stoked her fury.

"Guards!"

Flush with anger, she was clearly on the verge of losing her infamous temper. So focused on yelling for the guards, she didn't notice that the needle had started glowing.

First it appeared to be touched by the slightest shaft of dusty sunlight, an impossibility given that we were in a windowless corridor. It shone brighter, starting to resemble a full moon. After a moment, it turned white and hurt the eyes to look directly at it.

"Wh-what did you do?"

Even now, she wasn't scared so much as haughty. She opened her mouth again, no doubt so she could release another barrage of threats, but I lost my patience. I held up a hand and she found herself speechless, to her great surprise.

"I put a stay on your reign over this land," I replied. "And while you enjoy the break—or not—you would do well to reconsider your approach." I took a step toward her. She took a reflexive step back despite herself. I let my disguise drop, just a little. My eyes became wider and turned from hazel to golden yellow. My mouth opened in a grin, revealing far too many razorlike teeth, several with suspicious black-red stains.

I continued, "I will be here when you wake." I edged forward even more and pressed her against the wall, a predator cornering its prey, forcing her to look into my eyes, which now had no resemblance to human eyes. "And I do not forget."

She exhaled in a snort and once again opened her mouth for yet another childish retort. But the needle was now glowing so bright as to sear your eyes looking at it. It flashed once, a blinding explosion of white light.

When the light faded, the princess was slumped against the wall. Everyone in the castle, including the village outside, had also fallen asleep.

And so they would stay, until outside magic interfered. I would have the time I needed to return home with my news. The council could make a considered decision. Bending over, I picked up the needle. It had done its job well and might come in handy again someday.

I returned home. The forest, sensing the castle's inactivity, crept eagerly toward it, consuming farmland in the process. When I shared my findings, the alfar and svartalfar were still ambivalent. They voted for no further course of action, as my spell had solved the problem for the time being, and the forest wights were happy with the additional territory.

The princess slept for a long, long time. Then an ambitious prince, whose cruelty rivaled hers, heard of the sleeping princess. He travelled long and far, from his formerly powerful kingdom ruined by debt. He fought his way through the forest. We tried to stop him at every step but failed, for he was not only vicious but cunning, and he escaped our traps. He made it to the castle and broke the curse, using a magical talisman of great strength he had stolen from a dragon's hoard. As the princess gasped a new breath, her father gasped his last, and she became the ruler of the kingdom—with the prince by her side, of course.

Together, they ruled with an iron fist. It took all our combined protective magics to keep the forest safe. The princess, now the queen, suspected that the wights of the forest, those witches and outcasts she despised so much, had something to do with her long sleep. The villagers suspected as much as well. For years, they left us offerings as encouragement to continue the fight.

The villagers and the court as well had their own suspicions about the origin of the king's illness. There were whispers that before his sudden illness, the princess had been spending more time in the castle library than usual and had even visited an apothecary. But whispers are just whispers, and they were never confirmed.

Eventually, the citizens of the kingdom revolted, tired of the treatment they had shouldered without complaint for too long. Some of the wights joined them. The kingdom was thrown into turmoil and dark, uncertain times.

That is how the alfar—you know them as the elves—came to rule, years upon years later. At first, they were acceptable rulers. The alfar are nothing if not impartial and just, with their focus on rules and traditions. And their long lives create political stability that human rulers often cannot provide. As the years went by, and your world and mine grew ever more separated, the humans became more and more scarce. Eventually, all the citizens of the kingdom were alfar or other wights.

The years continued to slip by, and this kingdom fell from grace. We are still more prosperous than many, but not prosperous enough for some, like the current princess, who bears a striking resemblance to that princess of old. She hungers for a *return to the golden days of yore, and would do anything to try and resurrect them.*

We sat in silence. I finally said, "Our version of the story goes a little differently."

Birke fixed those unblinking eyes on me. "Oh? How so?"

"Well, there are a few minor changes . . . The princess is good, and you're an evil witch who curses her at birth out of jealousy."

She sniffed with the merest hint of derision. "Of course. It's so much easier to sympathize with youth and beauty over age and wisdom."

"So . . . do you ever wish that you hadn't interfered?"

She thought before answering, then spoke slowly when she replied. "To tell the truth, I'm not sure. There's no way to know what would have happened if I hadn't. She may have ruled for a short time before being overthrown. As cunning as she was, her flaws made her weak and easy to manipulate. The prince made her harder to deal with. Or she may have lived a long life and borne children, creating an even darker turn of events."

We sat in silence again, then she shrugged. "At any rate. Are you ready for more training before you sleep?"

I groaned—I was hoping we'd done enough for one day. Resigned to my fate, I hauled myself to my feet for another round.

# CHAPTER THIRTEEN

We continued with the same routine over the next two days. After waking, Birke had me chop firewood or do other chores. I cleaned, sweeping the wooden floor in the cottage and dusting off the shelves of Birke's relics. In addition to the slate she'd used to teach me the runes, there were various rocks and crystals, assorted knick-knacks, and several bones, most shiny white but a few still sporting rust-colored stains. For my part, I tried not to think about what (or who) the bones used to belong to. Once I finished my chores, we'd eat breakfast and launch into training. We went over the runes until I could throw both of them with ease and hold them for several minutes without breaking a sweat.

I also finally got to have a real bath—sort of. I could see why Birke had put it off before. It involved hauling in buckets of snow, melting them over the fire until they were scathing hot, and pouring them into a washbasin, one by one. The individual buckets of water were near boiling when I poured them in, but by the time there was enough water to wash in, it was barely on the warm side of tepid. Hot water or no, I scrubbed myself from head to toe and felt like a new woman when I got out.

I washed my clothes as best I could, too. After all, it didn't do any good to remove my eye-watering body odor if I was still wearing clothes that reeked of dirt, sweat, blood, and who knows what else. The whole process took close to three hours. Birke, ever the taskmaster, only let me do it after I'd shown her I could hold an Algiz shield up for a full fifteen minutes while her furry friend rammed it, searching for weaknesses. Even then, she still made me practice Thurisaz while waiting for the buckets of snow to melt.

On the third day, after breakfast, I stood up and stretched. Finally, I felt like I had a small chance of coming out the other side of this little quest in (mostly) one piece. I was relatively clean, I had on relatively clean clothes, and I could do fancy magical stuff I'd had no idea was even possible a week ago. I was starting to fancy myself a ragamuffin superhero.

"So," I said, "what's on the agenda for today? More runes?"

Birke, browsing through her odd dusty relics, shook her head. "There are many other runes to learn. You have twenty-two more to go before you've learned the basics. Then, you can layer them to combine their effects and create bindrunes, which produce a whole new outcome. I would like to teach you all of them, but we don't have time." She returned the large chunk of crystal she'd been holding to the shelf and turned to face me. "Assuming you survive this encounter, you can return for more training later."

"Is that part of our, um, arrangement?" I didn't want to offend her, but I also didn't want to get in over my head. The less favors I owed to mysterious forest-dwelling witches with pointy teeth and animal eyes, the better.

Birke nodded. "Occasional training is part and parcel of being one of Mine. Which, as we've covered, you became when I saved your life. But that's a matter to discuss later," she continued, waving a hand to brush it aside. "Today, we need to continue your training. Come here."

I crouched next to her by the fire. Her eyes looked more orange than yellow in the flickering light, which also tinted her pale skin gold. "We've already established you don't have a particular elemental affinity. *But* that doesn't necessarily mean you can't use the elements. Fire will be the most useful for you to learn right now, so we'll start there, and see how you take to it."

She pulled up the sleeve of her dress and dug her hand deep into the flames. My hand shot out instinctively to stop her, but it was too late. Expecting to see blisters and burns, I cringed. But when she pulled out a handful of red-hot embers, her arm and hand appeared to be fine. There was some soot and ash on her skin, but no burns. "Close your eyes," she commanded.

Hoping that this wasn't going to be another trial-by-fire test—literally—I complied. I felt her take my right hand and hold it over the embers. Their heat tickled my palm.

"Now," she instructed, "picture the embers in your mind. Try to get a good feel for their location based on the heat. Once you can see what they look like in your mind's eye, reach out with your energy."

Eyebrows knitted together, I tried my best to follow her instructions. I pulled at my energy and directed it to my right hand, the way I had when throwing runes. To my surprise, I could sense the fire.

"I . . . I can feel it. It's like I'm shining a light on it. I can see it in my mind and . . ." I paused, trying to articulate what it felt like. "I can feel something in the embers . . . answering my own energy. It's like a call and response."

"You're feeling the heart of the embers. Reach out with your energy and touch it. Try to draw it back to you." I felt warmth wash over my hand as she continued, "Now, turn your hand over and open your eyes."

I flipped my hand over and drew it back toward me, palm now facing up. Opening my eyes, I saw a tiny flame flickering in my cupped hand, hovering just above my palm. Unable to contain myself, I gave a little gasp of surprise and delight. In response, the flame dropped into my palm and went out. My delighted gasp turned into a small shriek of pain.

"It burned me!" I showed her the reddening circle on my palm, indignant.

She nodded, a small smirk playing at the corners of her mouth. "Yes. Fire does that. She stood up to dump the embers back into the fire and brushed her sooty hand off on her apron. "Since you don't have an inborn affinity for fire, you'll never be able to create it from scratch. But you can learn to control it, with practice. I want you to practice drawing a flame out of this fire, holding it in your palm, and directing it. See if you can get out the door without it going out. Once you've done that, try to control the fire enough to burn a specific twig on one of the logs outside. And once you've done *that*, come back inside and practice with these."

She rustled around in her apron pockets and pulled out a piece of flint and a small oval of metal as wide as my hand. I took the flint from her, but as my fingers brushed the metal, they burned with a familiar unpleasant tingle.

"You're giving me iron?" I yelped, snapping my arm back to nurse the singed fingers.

Birke blinked. "Oh. I did not think of it. I suppose the

steel *would* be a problem for you. Here." She dug around in her apron pockets again. "Wrap this around it." She pulled out a scrap of leather to demonstrate. The metal oval had one flat, smooth side and one side twisted in a spiral. Birke gripped the twisted side with the leather, like a pot holder. She took the flint from me and struck it against the metal in a smooth motion. An answering shower of sparks fell. Then she slid her hand out of the leather-and-steel contraption and handed the items over.

I took them from her, giving her a suspicious look. I'd assumed Birke was some kind of elf-related creature, despite the way she talked about them. But if she wasn't sensitive to iron at all, what *was* she? I guess it didn't matter at this exact moment, but it was still a little unsettling. I asked another, more pertinent question: "What if my knuckles touch it?"

She shrugged. "Don't let your knuckles touch it, then." I narrowed my eyes, making a face, and she relented a bit. "I will see if I can find some gloves for you. But you may not always have gloves available. If it comes down to an iron burn or saving your life, I would presume you would take your life, yes?"

I rolled my eyes and grunted. "I *guess*. So that's my homework for today, then?"

"Yes. You need to teach yourself to find the heart of the fire and manipulate it. You'll have an adequate grasp on that once you can carry a flame outside without it going out. You'll be able to manipulate even the smallest of fires, like a spark." She nodded at the tools. "As you can imagine, being able to create and wield fire from even a tiny spark could come in very handy."

I stared at the fire and the tools in my hands. I'd only been up an hour and I was already overwhelmed by my to-do list for the day.

"Wait," I said as she walked over to the door. "You're giving me instructions like you won't be here today."

She glanced back at me. "I won't. I need to keep an eye on my forest and see what I can learn. You'll be fine. Just don't burn my cottage down." She winked at me, but her tone was entirely serious. I wasn't quite comfortable with being able to tell if she was joking or not. But then, nothing about this situation was exactly comfy. At any rate, it was too late to ask follow-up questions. With a gust of cold air, she was gone. I turned back to face the fire.

"Well," I muttered under my breath, "it's just you and me now, buddy. Let's see what we can do."

Several hours later, I was sporting several singe marks on my clothes and countless tiny burns all over my arms. The silver lining was that I'd been able to pull the fire onto my hand multiple times and had even made it out the door. A few tries later, I'd kept the fire under control enough to burn just *one* twig on a log. Granted, I may have turned a few logs into piles of ash in the process, but nobody ever said learning new things was easy.

Satisfied with my progress, I went back inside and took up the flint and striker again, being careful not to burn myself on the steel. Holding them the way Birke had shown me, I knocked them together, but I wasn't rewarded with the shower of sparks she'd created. It took several rounds of practice before I was able to strike it in *just* the right way to get the same results. Of course, then I realized I needed to be able to do it one-handed, leaving the other hand free to manipulate the flame. Sighing with frustration and sweat beading on my forehead, I propped the striker against the fireplace just so. That way, not only did I have a hand free, I wasn't at risk of hurting myself.

After about an hour of trying without success, all the while growing more and more irritated, I finally got some results. With a lot of effort, I managed to pull a spark onto my open hand and give it enough energy to create a small flame, without it exploding into a fireball. Sitting back on my heels, I stared at the tiny flame dancing on my palm. Using the skills I'd been working on all day, I made it dance across my fingertips, back to my palm, then grow in size until it was six inches tall and as wide as my palm. A satisfied smile spread over my sweaty face.

My triumph was short-lived, though. The door creaked open, and. Birke swept into the room over to me. I didn't say anything, just held up the flint in one hand and the flame in the other. It was still going strong, having only flickered a tiny bit when I'd looked up. She looked from one to the other and nodded her approval, then reached out and scooped the flame up from my hand. She stared at it for a second before waving her other hand over it, extinguishing it, and turned back to me.

"I have bad news."

I didn't reply, leaning back against the wall to get a better look at her face. I was too tired to get worked up. And as bratty as it sounds, I was a little annoyed I didn't get to savor the victory that took me all day (and an annoying amount of pain) to earn.

"According to my sources, we have even less time than I'd thought. Gwyneira has been calling emissaries from the other kingdoms to the castle. They start arriving the day after tomorrow. She's gathering them for an announcement." Birke sat down in her chair and folded her hands in her lap. "Based on what I know about her and her methods of building alliances, there is a good chance she'll be making a public show of force. That could very well include executing her brother."

I blew a breath out through my teeth, sighing in frustration. "So we don't even have a full week to train."

She shook her head. "I think your best bet at getting inside the castle is while her people are dealing with all the new arrivals. That means tomorrow is our last day of training."

Panic squeezed my chest. "B-but," I spluttered, "that's not enough time! I only just got the hang of making fire!" I dropped the flint to put my head in my hands.

Birke touched my shoulder in a show of almost-bordering-on affection. "You are already far better prepared than you were a few days ago. I would hazard to say you are far better prepared than you would have been if you had approached the castle without meeting me." She withdrew her hand and the chair creaked as she stood up. "Wallowing will do nothing. If you are determined to complete your quest, this is the way. We will train tomorrow and work on perfecting what you've learned as much as possible. You will leave the morning after."

My vision clouded by tears, I ran a hand through my hair. She was right. I'd already known I was probably walking straight into suicide-by-elf. Even if I was still under-equipped, I was a hell of a lot better off than I'd been even a few days ago. Sniffling, I brushed the tears away. "You're right," I said, standing up. I exhaled again, this time in determination. "What do we do now?"

Pleased that I had pulled myself together, she graced me with a smile. "We train some more, of course." Why had I bothered asking?

For the next several hours, we practiced my skills with the fire. My luck with creating sparks with the striker propped against the fireplace gave me an idea. With a little of Birke's help, we fashioned a holster of sorts for the striker. That makes it sound fancy, but really, we just strapped some leather around it. I could now tie it around my hips, smooth side facing out. No chance of burning my knuckles, and this way, I could hold the flint in my left hand and catch the sparks with my right. Birke seemed pleased with my ingenuity, and it certainly made it easier to create fire on the move, which gave me a tactical advantage. The last thing I wanted was to be run through with a sword a second time while I was trying to find my fire-starting tools.

That night, while we rested for a moment after dinner, I stared into the fire. I was grimy, despite the bath I'd just taken that morning, and exhausted. Looking into the bright flames reminded me of their opposite, that space between the worlds I'd touched when crossing through the Slip.

"Birke?"

"Mmm?"

"Do you know who caused the Slip?"

"Who *caused* it?" She sounded amused, as though it were a ludicrous idea. "What gave you the idea that someone caused it?"

"I mean . . . it didn't just happen. There had to be a reason." I tried not to sound desperate. "Right?" It had been the turning point in my life. I needed a reason.

Glancing over my shoulder, I saw her shrug and watch me with her usual inscrutable expression. "Is there a reason that earthquakes happen? Or the tides? The worlds do what they do. It has always been that way."

Something about staring into the fire, thinking about the impossible task ahead of me, was making me reminisce. Or maybe it was recently facing down death. That makes a girl think. "You know, my mom died because of the Slip. There were riots. People were afraid. Angry. I left her alone . . . the last time we talked, we were fighting because of it. She was my only family." My voice cracked a little. "She died because of me." It was something I'd never admitted out loud before.

Birke's response was not unsympathetic. "Forces larger than you were at play. Blaming yourself makes no sense. And, for better or for worse, you are an orphan. I believe that may be another reason our paths crossed. Orphaned children are my domain. If you were not an orphan, we may not have met."

I snorted, irritation replacing my grief over old wounds. "I'm not a child, Birke."

The now-familiar peals of laughter echoed around the small room. "You are to me."

The next day was a blur of practice. We barely rested after lunch and dinner before jumping back into the fray. The morning was dedicated to Algiz, the afternoon to Thurisaz, and the evening was focused on fire. Dire situation aside, I had to admit that running around with a fireball in my hand *did* make me feel like a total badass. I wasn't a master at any of these things yet, but I was at least proficient.

The night before my departure, I couldn't sleep. I stared at the ceiling, my thoughts chasing each other around in my head. I was alone in the cabin, as Birke was out hunting again. Logan, my best friend. The children, taken from their families. This bizarre adventure, complete with a talking fox, a dryad, and a near-death experience. Gwyneira, the catalyst for the whole thing. What would it be like to go back home, knowing that all of this was so close?

Eventually, I lost myself in a night of restless sleep and short dreams, all stressful. Logan killed before my eyes, returning home empty-handed, Rosa crying. I woke up gasping, thrashing around in the blankets and almost rolling off the bed. The sun was up. Birke was turning meat on the fire, as usual, and raised an eyebrow at my sudden—and loud—wakening. It was go time.

Once the food was ready, Birke took her portion and disappeared outside. I could only assume she was making arrangements of some sort. After I finished eating, I packed up my backpack and looked around the tiny room that had been my home for the last few days. To my surprise, I found myself feeling almost fond of it. It wasn't much, but it also wasn't the worst place I'd ever stayed, not by a long shot.

Birke returned while I was running through my mental checklist for the fourth time, making sure I hadn't forgotten anything. "Are you prepared?"

I swallowed. "I guess so."

She held the door open for me. I spared one last glance at the warm, safe cottage and its welcoming fire. Outside, I paused and looked to her for instructions, uncertain where to go next. "So . . . which way should I start walking?"

She scoffed, amused. "You thought you were going to walk to the castle? That would take another day, and you'd risk getting lost again. No, Tania. This is my forest and I travel through it as I please." She took me by the arm, just above my elbow, and grasped hard. I didn't have time to cry out in protest before the trees around us blurred. Mere seconds later, we came to a jarring stop. I threw out my arms to make sure I didn't face-plant and bent over with my hands on my knees. I'd been hit with a terrible case of motion sickness.

"A little warning next time, maybe?" I gasped between retches.

Her expression was one of dispassionate curiosity. "I always forget it's not the same for others. My apologies." She turned to point. "The servant's entrance to the castle is that way. Remember, the staff won't be susceptible to a glamour. My suggestion is to shift. Make yourself appear like a servant. The entrance should be easy to get through, as most of the available staff will be greeting emissaries." She gave a pointed look at the steel that I'd strapped around my waist in our makeshift halter. "You'll want to remove that."

Surprised at my oversight, I untied the leather strip, wadded the steel up in the leather, and stuck it in my pocket. Birke glanced me over, head to toe, and reached out to straighten my jacket. She even bent down to tuck one of my pant legs inside my boot, an oddly motherly gesture coming from her. "There. Now I believe you are ready." She stepped back and waved a hand toward the castle. "Tell Logan that my debt to him is repaid."

Gulping, I took a half step forward. I turned back to say good-bye, but she was already gone. Figures.

Taking a second to calm my nerves, I pictured an elf in my mind and focused on shifting. Muscles tore and reknitted and bones groaned as I grew a few inches taller, my cheekbones became more prominent, and my ears became pointy. Luckily, shifting was easier here than back home. Finished with the process, I brushed my ears to make sure they were elfish enough. I hoped that my twenty-first-century clothes weren't too unusual for a servant. Unable to stall anymore, I took a deep breath and walked toward the castle, praying that Logan was still alive and the children were unharmed.

# CHAPTER FOURTEEN

Ten short minutes later, I was at the servant's entrance. Nobody was even guarding it in all the excitement. People were bustling in and out in a steady stream. I fell in step with a group of staff and kept my head down. If you act like you belong, everyone assumes you do. And then, I was inside. I kept in line with the group for a few paces before peeling off to a side hallway.

The first thing I noticed was that this place was *huge*. It's not like I was expecting anything else. I'd seen it was a friggin' castle. But once I was past the first hurdle and inside without incident, I looked around and realized just *how* enormous it was. The walls were made of slate-gray boulder-sized bricks. The high ceilings were covered in gauzy curtains of cobwebs. I turned down another hallway. It was narrower, but still wide enough for four people to walk abreast. The castle's grandeur was tainted by the musty smell of mildew and damp stone that hung heavy in the air. Flickering torches on the walls completed the atmosphere.

Checking behind me to make sure I wasn't being followed, I dropped my disguise. The tiny pops and cracks echoed off the stone. Shifting had never been my strongest point, and I needed to save as much energy as I could. My ears pricked for oncoming strangers, I continued down the hallway and wondered how the hell I was going to find Logan. Smaller hallways branched off to my left and right, and I quickly realized how lost I was. Time to stop for a moment and figure out a plan.

Logan was, I assumed, in a dungeon of some sort. Dungeons were usually in the basement. It followed that, with any luck, if I headed downstairs at any given opportunity, I would run into it sooner or later. I hoped, anyway. I took one set of stairs down and continued on my way.

The walls grew cold and slimy, with spotty patches of green-gray lichen clinging for dear life in the space between the stones. The musty odor grew stronger. I turned a corner, then spun on my heel to duck back the way I'd come. Two armed guards stood in front of a large metal gate. Each one was holding a six-foot-tall pole tipped with a vicious foot-long blade ringed with sharp barbs at its base. I did *not* want to tangle with one of those.

Leaning against the wall to catch my breath, I weighed my options, listening for approaching guards to make sure I wasn't caught unawares. I could try attacking with fire—there were plenty of torches to pull from. I still had the flint and steel in my pocket, too. That might be better off as a last resort, though. I could try to draw them out and disarm them, using the runes, then escalate to fire if things got bad enough. Having decided that was a reasonable plan of action, I stepped out again, this time with purpose. Shifting my hands into clawed weapons, I strode toward the guards.

The sudden sound of gloved hands clapping behind me interrupted my march into battle. I whirled around to face it, caught off guard and confused. Metal clattered on stone as the guards dropped their weapons and grabbed me. I cried in surprise as they lifted me off my feet. The source of the clapping became apparent as the hooded woman from my dreams stepped out from the shadows, surveying me with an amused smile dancing on her lips.

"Well *done*," she said. Her voice was cold, cutting; it matched the cruelty in her smile. "I'll be honest, I didn't expect you to make it this far." She waved a hand at the guards, and they brought me closer. I squirmed, desperate to get away but unable to find leverage—not surprising given that my feet were flailing a solid foot off the ground. She circled me, savoring the moment, pulling off one of her gloves finger by finger as she did so. Once she had examined me from all angles, she turned to face me again and reached out her hand. Long, delicate fingers brushed one side of my face, then the other. She grabbed my chin and forced me to look at her, with a steely grip that didn't match the delicacy of her hand.

"I'm sure you have *plenty* of questions," she said, freezing me in place with her glacial stare. "Don't you worry your pretty little head." She accented each of the last three words with a condescending pat on my head. I wanted to spit in her face, but her grip had forced my jaw shut. "We'll have a wonderful little ladies' chat later, all right? But right now, I have duties to attend to." A slow, broad grin spread over her face. Gwyneira's teeth weren't pointed like Birke's, but her smile was as predatory as the forest witch's. I gulped despite myself.

"I do so love politics." Spinning on her heel, she swept off down the hallway, shouting over her shoulder at the guards. "Take her things and search her for weapons. Put her next to my brother, they can catch up on old times." She laughed as if she'd told a wildly entertaining joke. The sound echoed around the hallway as she strode off, distorting until it sounded demonic.

The guards turned around and carried me, feet still dangling, through the heavy metal gate into a long hallway of cells, most of them occupied. The stench hit me full in the face, making me gag—misery and filth mixed with moldy hay and cold stone. They stopped at the second to last cell. The guard on my right loosened his grip, freeing one hand to grab his keys and unlock the door. The other one took a hand off me to cut the straps of my backpack. They threw me headfirst into the cell before I had a chance to use their distraction to my advantage. I had to tuck and roll to keep from being injured on the rough stone floor, rolling right into a pile of wet hay. Furious, I sat up, bits of straw clinging to my hair and face, to see the guards standing outside, pointing and laughing at me.

They turned and walked off down the hallway, their laughter mixing with the prisoner's pleas for release, or more food or water. I stood and brushed myself off, trying to get the hay out of my hair and off my face, and looked around. The cell was minuscule. If I lay down on that pile of gross hay, my head and feet would touch the door and the opposite wall. The only light came from the sputtering torches in the hallway. I looked out the door to make sure the guards were out of sight. Satisfied I wasn't being watched, I stretched out my arms toward the closest torch, trying to get at the fire.

After a few tries, I gave up. It was almost two feet away from my fingertips, even when I stretched with all my might. That was probably intentional, unless there was a special high-security prison for each magical affinity. As I pulled my arm back inside, my bare wrist brushed the metal bars. I grunted in pain and jumped back, a tiny red streak appearing where my skin had touched the metal.

"Mother*fuckers*," I muttered to myself. "They put me in a cage with an iron door?"

A laugh that morphed into a scraping cough echoed from the cell next to mine. "Tania?" a hoarse voice whispered.

I knew that voice. I pressed myself as close as I could to the door, making sure none of my bare skin touched it, and whispered back.

"Logan? Is that you?"

More coughing, followed by a grunt of pain. "Yeah, it's me. Are you okay?"

"I could ask you the same thing. You sound like hell."

"I'm . . . I'm not doing so hot." A slow inhale rasped, an attempt to breathe in without setting off another coughing fit. "She's been having the guards rough me up every now and then, for fun. But they've also got me bound in iron. I think I'm getting sick."

I leaned back against the stone wall, closing my eyes and biting my lip to keep from crying. "Logan, this is my fault."

"Nah, Tania. I chose to come here with you. I chose to lead the Hunt away. I think some part of me knew that I need-ed some closure." The wry smile was apparent in his voice. "I guess I'm getting that, huh?"

I glared at the wall between us. "Don't talk like that. I'm getting us both out of here. And the kids, too. You just wait."

"I don't know if I've ever told you this, but your stubborn-ness, while frustrating at times, is one of the things I admire most about you."

I sighed and changed the subject so he'd stop with the gallows talk. "I found the White Woman. Birke."

His voice perked up. "Oh? Did she help?"

"Yeah. Quite a bit. In fact, she says her debt to you is re-paid . . . actually, now I owe *her*."

"What do you mean?"

"Weeeelllll." I dragged it out, stalling while I found the right words. I knew he wasn't going to like this. "Her great furry folk or whatever found me, because Reynard put out the word I was looking for her. But they happened to find me just after I'd been"—I took in a deep breath and spit it out all at once—"stabbed-in-the-stomach-by-some-guards."

He inhaled sharply and the chains clinked as he moved, followed by a second gasp of pain. I couldn't *believe* they'd bound him in iron. "You got stabbed?"

"Yeah. But I'm okay, because she healed me. She says I'm one of Hers now." I shrugged, then realized he couldn't see that, so I tried to force the casualness into my voice instead. "I mean, it can't be all that bad, right? Besides, she taught me a lot of new things, and she said she'll teach me more if I survive this whole mess." I laughed in spite of myself.

He was quiet for so long I thought he might have fallen asleep or passed out. "Logan?"

"I'm here . . . It's not bad per se, but it's serious stuff, Tania. Being under her wing is a pretty big benefit, though, so there's that."

I nodded. "Heaven knows we need all the help we can get."

A clanging reverberated down the hallway, followed by footsteps, hushing us both. The stomping implied heavy boots and armor, while the lighter set of footsteps gave me a solid guess who was coming to visit, and I wasn't looking forward to it. I scrambled back from the door.

Sure enough, a few seconds later Gwyneira stood in front of my cell, her gloved hands on the bars. "There's our newest guest!" She motioned for the guard behind her to open the door. He pulled an old-school ring of keys from his belt, his thick gloves protecting him from the iron door as he swung it open. Gwyneira floated through and looked around the tiny cell, smiling. "How are you finding our castle so far?"

I made a face—it might have been childish, but it was my first reaction. "I've seen nicer."

She smirked at one of her guards, her eyebrow quirked as if I'd told a joke. Taking in the hay in my tangled hair, my torn jacket, worn jeans, and beat-up boots, she said, "Have you now? That comes as a surprise. Judging by your appearance, this is well above your standards." The guards chuckled right on cue, trained lapdogs with pikes.

I sneered. "Why are you here? Don't you have things to do?"

"Oh, don't you worry. I've taken care of my duties. In fact, they're what brought us together. That, and incredible stupidity on both your and my brother's part." She shrugged and looked at the ceiling. "He was never the best strategist. That's why I wound up in charge and he wound up banished."

I spat at her feet. "Your brother is a better person than you could ever hope to be."

Unruffled, she looked down at the wet splotch on the floor, then glanced over her shoulder at the guards and tilted her head toward me. In response, they grabbed me by the shoulders, forcing me up against the wall, while she looked on, mocking me with her smile.

"My dear," she said, tapping her finger on the tip of my nose. "I came here to offer you a deal. While not anything special for *our* kind"—she gestured at the guards, herself, and the castle around her—"your talents are quite intriguing. Think about it," she continued, spreading her hands in a placating gesture and looking around my cell. "With you at my side, assisting in my new trade, you could be living in the best rooms of this castle, helping to create a whole new realm."

I screwed up my face to spit at her again, but one of the guards grabbed my mouth and held it shut. Instead, I stared at her with all the disgust and contempt I could muster.

She tsk-tsked, sounding for all the world like a bored nanny dealing with an unruly child. "Let's try that again." She stepped closer, ice-blue eyes boring holes in my head. "What would it take to make the offer more appealing? I am not an unkind person. I could offer to let my brother go, unharmed . . . well, not harmed further." She smirked again, and I hated her more than I'd ever hated anything. "That is *quite* the generous offer."

My eyes widened, wondering if she was serious. Logan coughed and spluttered in protest with a weak, "No, don't . . . you can't . . ."

Gwyneira rolled her eyes. "Are you going to let *him* make this decision for you?" She gave the tiniest nod at the guard holding my mouth shut. He let go, and she stepped closer still; I could feel her breath on my face. Her eyes were all I could see, staring into mine. My vision blurred and a buzzing noise sounded in my ears. "Wouldn't that be nice? You'd live here, and never want for anything. Logan would be safe. Nothing to worry about."

The noise vibrating in my skull made it hard to think. *Was* it a good idea? Getting Logan out alive . . . that would be a victory . . . and I couldn't go home right now, anyway. There was a witch hunt out there with my name on it. Would it be so bad to stay here? A memory tickled at the back of my head, but the buzz drowned it out. Gwyneira was still talking, but I was trying to focus on my thoughts and couldn't make out much.

The memory came back, crying for attention. I reached toward it, pulling it closer. In my mind's eye, Alejandro popped into full Technicolor view, with the look of heartbreaking wonder when he'd seen my powers. Rosa's emotional rollercoaster when she found out he'd been taken. The red eyes of the woman in the coffee shop. Those kids had families. They deserved to be with them.

I shook my head, knocking it on the stone wall behind me in an effort to clear it. The pain drove away the last of the humming and blurred vision. "The children. What about the children?" It felt like I was talking around peanut butter, but I forced the words out anyway.

Gwyneira, interrupted midsentence, stepped back. "The children? I'm afraid they're non-negotiable."

"You're keeping them here no matter what?" The words were coming easier now.

She stared at me for a moment, tight-lipped, before nodding. I jutted my chin up at her, defiant. "Then no deal."

"But *dear*," she replied, moving closer again and locking eyes with me. The humming started again at the corners of my attention. "Be *reasonable* . . ."

No longer held back by the guard's hand, I spat full in her face. The distracting noise disappeared and she stopped in her tracks, the glob of saliva running down her cheek, leaving a wet trail. One eye twitched, the only show of emotion as she wiped her face, stared at her fingers, and then flicked them. She took a moment before replying.

"Well. I *had* hoped we'd be able to work together. But now," she said, with a sad sigh that ended in a theatrical pout, "I see that's impossible. No matter. You can become a part of my demonstration tomorrow. We'll show the representatives of other kingdoms how I handle subjects who defy banishment and this new type of . . . interloper." She paused with a hand on the door. An icy smile, one that didn't reach her eyes, flashed on her face. "Between you two and the other demonstration, I think it will be *quite* some time before anyone thinks to trifle with my kingdom."

At her signal, the guards dropped me. One of them kicked me in the gut before he walked out. Once again, I found myself facedown in the hay, but this time I was gasping for air, adding injury to insult. I struggled to my feet so I could peer through the door and see if they were gone. Gwyneira's silver cloak was barely visible, fluttering as she walked out the main gate. The coast was clear.

Rubbing my stomach to ease the ache, I whispered, "Logan, did you hear all that?"

He grunted in acknowledgment.

"What other demonstration is she talking about? She has plans for those kids. I think they're a big part of it." I tapped my head against the stone wall in frustration. "There has to be a way out of here."

The chains rattled. "I don't know if there is, Tania." His voice was frayed in a way I'd never heard before.

Ignoring the defeat in his voice, I paced my cell. We had until tomorrow—probably tomorrow morning—to get ourselves and the kids out. I didn't know where the children were. Assuming we could actually escape, it was only a matter of time before the guards would start searching for us. We'd have to find the kids and get out of the castle before that happened. After *that*, we had to cross the woods to the Slip before Gwyneira's soldiers tore the forest apart looking for us, or we ran into something even worse.

Put like that, it did sound a little impossible. But I'd be damned if I wasn't going to go out swinging. I sighed, running my hands through my hair in frustration, untangling the knots out of habit. I rested my hands on my hips, where I noticed a lump in my pocket. I started. How had I forgotten that? I still had Birke's flint and steel in my pocket. There *was* a potential escape route after all.

I stuck my head out the door as far as I could without the iron burning me. The guards were at the gate, not even bothering to patrol the dungeon.

"Logan," I hissed, "I think there might be a way out after all."

"Mmm. What's that?"

My words were fast and quiet. I hoped the guards couldn't hear me. "I have what I need to start a fire, and Birke taught me how to manipulate flames. With enough time, I might be able to melt the bars or something so we can get out."

He sounded more optimistic, but still cautious. "Tania, that'll take hours. You'll need to stop to recharge, or when they do patrols. That's about every three hours, by my best guess. They also haven't brought today's 'food,' which is another interruption. If they see *any* sign the gate is being tampered with, they'll put you in irons, too."

"Yeah, I know. That's why I gotta get started now."

After checking to make sure the guards still hadn't moved, I stepped back from the door. Holding the steel carefully so I didn't burn myself, I struck the flint on it, causing the familiar shower of sparks, then pulled those into a small flame in my other hand. I inspected the lock, figuring it was an obvious target. I actually didn't know if I could get the fire hot enough to melt metal. It would need to be either supremely hot, or held on the lock for a long time. Both would be draining.

Closing my eyes, I pulled up every ounce of energy I could and focused it all on one tiny point. It worked: the flame in my palm had turned into a white-hot pinpoint that hurt my eyes. Staring at it, I nudged it to the tip of my finger, creating a miniature blowtorch. Not too shabby.

Satisfied this would do the job, I checked for guards one last time before going to town on the lock. Progress was slow, but half an hour later, it was visibly weaker. I stopped, panting. Logan was right—it *was* exhausting. But the progress was promising. I whispered the good news to him and asked him to keep an ear out for me.

I had to take a one-hour break after every thirty-minute welding session. After a couple of rounds, I was struggling to keep my eyes open. I leaned against the wall, dozing, when the telltale stomp of boots approached down the hallway. I gave the door a wary glance, hoping they wouldn't need to open it—they'd notice something was off. Lucky for me, the guard just sneered at me. He held out a bowl and said, "Here's your dinner," then dumped its contents on the ground through the grating and dropped the bowl with a clatter. I closed my eyes again, ignoring his raucous laughter at his own joke. It didn't smell like something I'd want to eat, anyway, even with a growling stomach.

In an attempt to keep Logan's spirits up, I'd been relaying my progress to him. It seemed to be working, especially as I neared my goal. Once I got out, I'd have to melt his lock in short order, so I'd need full energy reserves. And then we still had to get past the guards, but either way, the progress was visible and it boosted both our moods.

I continued working on the lock until I almost gave myself third-degree burns in my clumsy exhaustion. I nodded off in that cursed pile of hay, meaning to sleep for just a couple of hours before continuing my work. Instead, I was startled awake what felt like a full night of sleep later by the loud rattling of a wrought-iron door creaking open.

# CHAPTER FIFTEEN

Groggy, I scrambled to my feet, thinking the guards had come into my cell. It was only after I was standing that I realized they'd opened the neighboring cell. Logan.

I rushed to the door, trying to get a good look at what was going on. All I could see were the backs of two guards at his door, with the sounds of another one rustling around inside his cell. Chains clanked as they hit the floor.

Words came, gruff and disdainful. "Come on, on your feet." The guards at the door parted to make way for the third guard, who was all but carrying Logan. The guard made no attempt to keep Logan's arms or lolling head from banging the cell door on the way out. Getting a good look at Logan felt like having the wind knocked out of me all over again. In the few days he'd been here, he'd acquired a puffy purple eye and a wicked-looking patch of scrapes on one cheekbone. Large, oozing welts encircled his wrists and lower arms. Dirty, torn clothes hung off his frame, his skin ashen underneath the grime and bruising.

"Logan!" I shrieked. He shifted his head to face me, but only slightly, his green eyes struggling to open all the way. "What did you monsters do to him?" The guards laughed at my impotent rage as I yelled at them from behind bars. Tears splashed down my face as one of them poked Logan in the ribs, watching for my reaction.

"Don't worry, love," one of them said, sneering at me as the other two carried Logan away. "We're just getting him properly attired. Gwyneira wants him wearing traditional royal garb. It'll make a better impression. You'll be joining him soon enough."

I gritted my teeth, trying to keep my angry tears under control enough to speak. "I. Am. Going. To. Kill. You."

He made a mock-scared face, then turned and followed the other guards down the hallway, still laughing. Panting with fury, I waited until I couldn't hear them anymore. A look down the hallway confirmed that they had left. Only one guard remained. If only I hadn't overslept! But there wasn't time for regret. This was the best chance I was going to get.

Digging deep inside myself, I pulled on my emotions as fuel. Rage, worry, fear—they were all there for the taking. Digging out the flint and steel from where I'd hidden them under the hay, I struck them together. My hands shook the first few times, but finally, a waterfall of sparks flew out. I grabbed at it with my mind, hard. Now holding a blazing foot-tall fireball, I double-checked to make sure the guard wasn't looking, then flung it at the lock.

Using my emotions as fuel was more effective than I'd imagined. The fireball clung to the door, sizzling. Tiny globs of metal dripped off, congealing on the stone floor, and the air became thick with the acrid smell of melting metal. Backing up against the wall, I covered my mouth with my arm.

A few minutes later, as the fumes were dissipating, the air wavered with heat, and the metal was still glowing white-hot. I didn't want to burn the hell out of myself and hinder my fighting abilities, so I had to wait for the fire to die out. To keep myself from fidgeting, I strapped the leather belt on and holstered the steel in it, then did a few practice strikes to make sure I hadn't lost the hang of it. I left the flint in my pocket, where it was easily accessible.

In an effort to calm my nerves, I did a last-minute inventory. I debated leaving my beloved leather jacket behind, but decided against it. It might slow me down a little, but it didn't hinder my access to the striker, and it could provide some protection. Either way, there was nothing useful in its pockets, and nothing, besides some lint, in my jean pockets, either.

But something in my right boot caught my eye. A small piece of rough brown leather was nestled between my thick sock and my jeans, impossible to notice unless I'd been looking for it. Pulling it out, I realized it was a flap of leather folded around—I opened it—a sewing needle. One as long as my pinkie finger, with a wicked-sharp point. The silver of the needle glistened with shades of blue and green, as though it had been dyed with an aurora.

Mouth agape, two memories flickered through my mind: Birke tucking my jeans into my boot; and her telling the Sleeping-Beauty-gone-awry tale, firelight moving shadows across her face.

Holy shit. The witch had slipped me her magic needle.

Talk about a game changer. *That* considerably improved our chances of getting out alive. A fresh wave of determination washing over me, I wrapped the needle and tucked the leather into my pocket. The dull end of the needle stuck out enough that I could easily grab it when the time came.

By now, the lock had finished melting. A weakened, ravaged mess was all that remained. Backing up until my heel touched the back wall of the cell, I squared my shoulders and took a running leap at the door, kicking it open.

No time to spare, I spun and ran down the hallway as fast as I could, drawing fire from the torches around me as I dashed by. The other prisoners watched, some even whooping and cheering me on. The guard couldn't miss the racket and unlocked the gate. Seeing me, his face flickered from confusion to fear. He tried to grab his pike. Too late. Kicking off the wall, I jumped at him and brought a streak of flame down across his face and body. His weapon hand blistered as he tried to shield himself, and he fell back, his mouth a tiny *o* of confusion and pain as he clutched his injured hand. I must have been quite the picture, dirty and disheveled, fire coming from either hand and fury all over my face.

"Wh-what the—" he stammered.

Determined not to prolong the fight, I closed in and held a fireball right by his face. As luck would have it, it was the guard who'd mocked me not even an hour earlier. Grinning, I leaned in to whisper to him.

"I told you I'd kill you."

I pushed the fireball in his face. He screamed and slumped to the floor, passed out from the pain. I hadn't *actually* killed him, but why not put the fear of God in someone if you have the chance?

I grabbed the ring of keys off his waist. What next? I still didn't know how to get to wherever I needed to go. An idea struck me. The people in here must hate Gwyneira as much as I did.

"Hey!" I barked to the prisoner in the closest cell. He was

standing close to his cell door, trying to watch the fight. He was the shortest elf I'd seen so far, stout, with an almost comically round nose.

"Yes, er, milady?" he squeaked in response.

"Where would a demonstration be held?"

"Oh," he said, smiling, glad to be of help, "that would be in the main ballroom, I suspect. You'll go out that hallway"—he pointed—"and take two rights, three lefts, and then another right at the suit of armor."

"Two rights, three lefts, another right at the suit of armor?" I repeated back to him. This was one time I definitely couldn't afford to get directions wrong.

He nodded. "Yes, milady."

"How many guards?"

"Just two, maybe three stationed at the ballroom entrance?"

I nodded at him as I turned to leave. "Thank you. I appreciate it." I tossed the key ring into his cell. "Get out while you can—and help the others out, too, will you?"

*Good.* I sprinted down hallways, following his instructions. The entire castle was deserted. She must have forced everyone to go to the ballroom. What an egomaniac. Approaching the suit of armor, I slowed down, wanting to make sure I got the jump on any guards. Lucky for me, the elf in the dungeon had actually overestimated. There was only one guard on duty, who looked bored and was trying to peek inside the ballroom to watch the proceedings. Hiding behind the corner, I struck some sparks and held a fire in my right hand, leaving the left free for throwing runes. As I stepped out from behind the suit of armor and dashed at the guard, I threw a Thurisaz rune at him before he'd had a chance to turn.

So *that's* what that looked like in action. Birke and I hadn't been able to practice it for real—she just kept telling me how dangerous it was. We'd only drilled my throwing the rune at the empty air. The rune flew at his face, pointy side out. As the wave of energy hit him, scratches appeared all over his face and hands, along with tears in his clothing and a dent on the sheath of his sword. He cried aloud, clutching his head—I could only imagine it was causing psychic anguish, too. I was on him in a heartbeat, unsheathing his sword and using the pommel to knock him out.

So far, things had been easier than I'd hoped. But I hadn't hit the hard part yet. I took a moment before entering the room to compose myself and shift into a generic elf disguise. My goal was to blend in long enough to put a plan into action. The steel was in its holster, and I touched my pockets to make sure the flint was in one, the magic sewing needle in the other. Armed in my own weird way, I cracked the massive door just enough to slide through.

I glanced around, taking my surroundings into account, but never for more than a second at a time. Everyone else's attention was rapt on the scene unfolding at the far end of the room, and staring at the guards would draw attention to myself. The ballroom was humongous, with an ornate throne on a hastily built stage. Since everyone was staring at the stage, I worked my way through the crowd in that direction.

Gwyneira was standing onstage, in the middle of giving a speech. Behind her to her left was Logan—cleaned and wearing clothes in the same style as hers, but in different colors. He wore a beautiful light-green tunic with vines embroidered around the edge and forest-green breeches. She was clad in a close-fit light-blue tunic with dark-blue twisting embroidery around the edges that mimicked the vines on Logan's tunic. The dress had side slits that revealed fitted dark-blue breeches matching the embroidery. The effect was striking. She looked regal, but could still move freely and was unencumbered by miles of tulle, unlike some other women present.

Behind her on her other side was a group of children, including—was it really him?—Alejandro. I thought I spotted the boy from the missing-child poster, too. There were ten or fifteen children, all told. Something was wrong with them, though. They were standing too still, not a hair out of place. No sign of curiosity or restlessness or intelligence, the light behind their eyes dulled.

The natural acoustics of the room amplified Gwyneira's every word. "We are *all* aware that there have been some changes as of late. The borders between the worlds are thin, in a way they haven't been for several lifetimes. We have mostly ignored this and continued about our day-to-day lives. I argue that is a mistake. This is an unprecedented opportunity. In the past, we have taken children, one or two at a time, or lured adults over. We used the humans as our playthings, or took them as lovers, and returned them when we grew bored of them. But"—she held up a hand, one finger raised—"why stop at one or two children? Tradition? *Pfft.*"

She waved her hand, dismissing the silly notion. "No. Now that the doors between worlds are wide open, there is no reason *not* to take what should be ours and use it as we please. And I have done just that." With a flourish, she gestured to the glassy-eyed children, still as mannequins. "In the past, we took one child at a time to satisfy our need for amusement or as a pet. But with passage so easy and their children so plentiful, can we not use them for more? I say yes."

Eyes on the crowd, she snapped her fingers. The children moved, as one, to stand in a circle around her and face the crowd, expressionless.

"Friends, these children are so pliable, I can control them all with ease. And if we take them when they are young, they will never know free will. They will be ours to control. Imagine! Soldiers and servants that never want for anything. They'll toil ceaselessly, never complain, and never ask for pay."

Murmurs stirred up around me, and it didn't sound like all the reactions were positive. Gwyneira continued, ignoring the crowd's unrest.

"Of course, since I concocted this plan and put it into action, we will tax each of these purchases accordingly." She smiled at the crowd. "You understand."

The muttering continued. She lifted her eyebrow, almost imperceptibly, at the guard closest to her. Several of the guards on stage pounded their pikes on the stage for silence. The crowd's chatter faded away.

"As you can see, allying yourself with me and my kingdom will continue to be a wise decision in the future." The picture of a beneficent ruler, she smiled at the crowd again, looking quite satisfied with herself. "But of course, politics are a complicated game. Sometimes, for whatever reason, people go back on their word. While you're all gathered here, I thought I would show you why that is *such* a terrible idea."

At the snap of her fingers, the two guards nearest Logan grabbed him by the shoulders. They forced him to the front of the stage and then to his knees. He stared out into the crowd, exhausted and resigned. I kept edging closer to the stage but moved faster now, not liking the direction this was headed.

"As some of you may remember," Gwyneira continued, "this is my brother, Logan. I banished him many years ago. The details aren't important. What is important is that even though he was exiled, he defied me. He came back, you see, bringing a"—she searched for the appropriate words to describe the indignity she'd suffered—"half breed cretin from the other world." Her voice grew louder, gaining a thread of hysteria. "They sought to unseat me. To defy my rule! But no." Her annoyed expression faded, replaced with a creepy-calm smile. "I, of course, thwarted their attempt. And as we all know, the punishment for trespassing while exiled is death."

Grinning that predatory smile that showed all her teeth, she snapped her fingers again. The guards turned Logan so he was facing the crowd sideways, in profile. From across the stage, a black-hooded guard with a massive axe approached.

By this point, I was as close to the stage as I could get. Do or die time. Or, as the case may be, both. Steeling myself, I shifted back to my normal appearance as I yelled at the top of my lungs.

"No! Stop!"

The crowd gasped and parted around me, everyone turning to see who was protesting. Gwyneira's head snapped around as she searched for the source of dissent, nostrils flaring. I dashed out in front of the stage, exposed. As her guards moved toward me and she stared down, disgusted and angry, I shouted again, hoping everyone in the room could hear.

"Gwyneira, I challenge you to a duel!"

# CHAPTER SIXTEEN

For a few seconds, the entire ballroom was dead silent. After that, the crowd erupted—talking and pointing at us. The guards kept walking toward me, some grim-faced, some laughing at the stupidity of my bold move. Gwyneira herself, however, hadn't moved at all. Her face was a frozen mask of rage, her eyes still fixed on me.

"Stop!" she said to her guards, holding up a hand. Her guards immediately complied, looking from her to me and vice versa. Pausing, she smoothed her tunic and regained her composure before addressing the crowd. "Obviously, dealing with this . . . miscreant . . . is far, *far* beneath my stature. But who am I to back away from a challenge to a duel and dishonor my name? No." Making a big show of being unconcerned, she smiled at the crowd again. "You will get to see firsthand how I deal with would-be usurpers."

In one graceful move, she leapt off the stage and approached me. Though her voice was calm, her face had bloodlust written all over it, eyes narrowed and mouth set. I wondered if I had thought this plan through. Too late to back out now.

I backed up a little. But instead of attacking, she turned to the crowd, a smile plastered on her face, and spoke again. "You all know the rules. Could you please move back and clear a space for us? Who will set the boundaries? Obviously, it cannot be one of my guards. We don't want to make the odds even *less* in her favor." She forced a laugh at her own joke. An aristocratic-looking elf toward the front of the crowd raised a hand, and she nodded at him. Coming forward, he addressed both of us.

"The boundaries of the duel will be this half of the ballroom, save the stage." He gestured at a spot where the crowd was forming. "If you cross that line, you will be disqualified and executed. If you involve another person, the consequences are the same. You are allowed to use whatever magic you have available. There will be assorted weapons in the middle of the fighting area, and you may use whatever you can from those. You will back away from each other until I call. Then I will count down to the start of the duel. Understood?"

I gulped, nodding and trying to remember all the rules. Gwyneira gave a curt nod as she spun on her heel and walked off. When we were about twenty-five feet apart, the elf yelled, "Stop!" A guard moved forward to place the weapons in the middle of the space between us. Gwyneira turned her back to me and I followed suit, my mouth dry and palms sweaty as the well-dressed elf counted down. I touched the needle again, making sure it was still there, and put my other hand on the flint. Might as well go in guns a-blazin'.

"Two . . . one . . . go!"

I spun around, facing her and backing away at the same time, as I tried to get a spark. My slick hands made me clumsy, and it was four or five heart-pounding seconds before the sparks showered out. I pulled the fire into my left hand, sticking the flint back in my pocket. That way, my right hand was free so I could use the needle if I had the chance. But how was I going to get close enough to her?

Meanwhile, Gwyneira was pacing closer, biding her time. When she saw the fire, her eyes widened in surprise, then set in determination. Cursing to myself, I realized I should have kept that as a strategic surprise. Oh well—if I'd tried to do it spur of the moment, I might not have been able to get a spark. As she drew closer, stalking me rather than rushing at me, she passed the pile of weapons. Barely giving it a glance, she snatched a small knife, twirling it in her fingers and sticking it in her belt. I hadn't even tried to approach the weapons. I figured a blade would probably slow me down. I hoped my decision was the right one. For every step she took toward me, I took one back, keeping a wary eye on the boundaries.

"What's the matter? Are you afraid of fighting someone with *real* power?" Now that she was within striking distance, she seemed to feel safe taunting me.

I ignored her jibes, watching her body language instead. She was trying to irritate me, keep my off my guard. That meant she was going to feint and—ah, there it was. She feinted left, then struck right, her knife in her outstretched hand, slashing at me. Having seen the attack coming, I jumped back and away, throwing just enough fire at her to singe her sleeve but not do any real damage. The crowd gasped.

"That's a neat trick you have there," she continued in her loud, mocking tone. "I have one, too." Her eyes still on me, she stuck her hand out before making a grasping motion and pulling it in. A globule of water, glowing slightly, congealed in her hand. I was expecting this to come into play, but not so soon . . . And where did that water come from?

Seeing my confusion, she cackled, the harsh and merciless laugh echoing around the room. "Oh, were you unaware? I have real power, like I said. My element is a part of me so I can draw from it any time I please." The blob quivered, then split into four smaller spheres. They shook, expanded, and solidi-fied into frozen spears. Each one was a foot long with a deadly tip, and they were all pointed at me.

I sprinted to the side, keeping an eye on her. With a single gesture, she sent the icy spears after me, still laughing. Circling her, I threw up an Algiz shield between us. The ice-blades shattered as they hit it and fell to the ground with a tinkling noise, then melted into harmless puddles of water. The crowd started murmuring again. Gwyneira was on the verge of losing her temper.

"You studied with the forest witch, hmm? She's the only one I know who uses that trick. I wonder"—she drew more water into her palm and flung an ice-knife at me—"how she'll feel"—another one flew at my face—"when I kill you." Yet an-other one. Each spear shattered before reaching me, though my shield was starting to wane. Keeping it and the fire going at the same time was hard. I needed to try and end this as fast as possible. Still circling her, I drew closer, hoping her anger would leave her distracted.

"And leave your body at her cottage door," she finished, throwing three rapid-fire ice-daggers at me. Once the last one shattered on my Algiz shield, I returned fire with . . . well, fire, followed by a Thurisaz rune thrown right at her face. After that, I backed away, coughing, unable to see what had struck true and what hadn't in the haze of smoke and steam.

Seconds later, the smoke started to clear. One of my fire strikes had seared her hand, leaving blisters. She must have dodged the rest. And she'd screamed right after I threw the

Thurisaz—it had struck true. Deep scratches covered her face, and her clothes hung in singed tatters.

Gwyneira was quite a different picture than she'd been twenty minutes ago, when she was calm, cool, and collected. Now, she was sweaty, covered in soot and grime, shaking with rage, her clothes in rags. Panting, she whirled around in frantic circles, trying to find me. The crowd was coughing in the smoke and steam.

"Enough!" she screamed at earsplitting volume when she spotted me. And then, in a blur, she was right in front of me. I'd wondered when she was going to finally whip out the elf superspeed. I tried to jump, but realized I'd backed myself up against the stage in the confusion. The same realization hit her, and she laughed as she came closer, knife drawn.

I poured all my remaining energy into my fire, flaring it three feet high and swiping wildly. The stench of burning hair made me cough, and her shrieks made it hard to concentrate. Thinking I had cover, I ducked under her left arm—but it turned out the flailing arm was a trap. Instead of letting me get away, she grabbed my arm with the same iron grip she'd used the day before, spun me around, and slammed me into the stage.

"I told you," she snarled, spittle flicking my face. "I'm the one with the power around here." Emphasizing her point, she pulled back the knife and drove it deep into my belly. I stared at her, biting my lip, determined not to give her the satisfaction of crying out. She stared down at me, a smirk playing on her lips. "You were doomed from the start. You could have *never* hoped to win a duel against me."

I checked to make sure my hand was free. "That's okay," I grunted through gritted teeth. "I never cared about winning the duel, anyway."

She only had a split second to stare at me, bewildered, before I drew the needle out of my pocket and slammed it into her neck. Screaming, she staggered backward, clutching her neck. What seemed like miles away, I could hear the crowd trying to figure out what was going on. I stumbled away from the stage, clutching the dagger that was still buried in my stomach up to the hilt and looking around for Logan.

"Logan!" I shouted. "Are you okay? Logan!" The room was now a mess of chaos, and I had no idea where he was.

A few seconds later, he was at my side. "Tania," he gasped, seeing the knife. He tried to prop me up but was too weak. Instead, we clung together, trying to hold each other up. He looked from me to Gwyneira. "What's going on?"

Gwyneira was several feet away, shrieking like a banshee. Pain, confusion, and anger had distorted her face, making it unrecognizable. It was no longer a mask of statuesque beauty; now, she was just a pissed-off egomaniac who'd been defied. Her hands were clamped around her neck as though she were trying to hold it together. Through the cracks in her fingers, I could see the needle pulsing with white light.

The light grew until I couldn't look at her anymore, and then it kept growing until it permeated the entire room. Groaning, I flung my arms over my eyes, and Logan followed suit. A loud clap sounded, after which the light vanished.

I peeked through my arms. Logan's sister had collapsed in a puddle, eyes closed, the needle still protruding from her neck. Standing over her was Birke, her homespun clothes contrasting with the dirty grandeur of the ballroom. Birke nudged Gwyneira with her foot and, when there wasn't a response, seemed to be satisfied that she was out cold. Looking up, Birke spotted me and Logan, still holding each other up and taking in the whole situation.

With a few short steps, she stood in front of us. "Aren't you two the picture of health," she said wryly, her eyes moving from Logan's bruises and welts to the knife sticking out of my stomach.

Logan glared at her. "I know you have an off sense of humor, but in case you didn't notice, Tania has a mortal wound. This is not the time for jokes."

Birke cocked her head as she looked at him, a smile playing on her lips. "Tania, come here," she said, waving me over. I took a faltering step or two, gritting my teeth to keep from wailing in pain. She put one hand on my shoulder, the other on the handle of the knife. With no warning, she pulled it out.

Logan cried out, "You'll kill her!"

Birke was now openly amused. "Did neither of you notice that Tania isn't bleeding?" She pointed to my wound with the knife she was now holding. "Did you forget she's under my protection?" she asked Logan. She raised her eyebrows at me. "Did you not tell him that?"

I ignored the questions and lifted my shirt. Sure enough, there was nothing but a thin silver line that matched the scar across my hips. And now that the knife was gone, the searing pain was gone, too, leaving only a bruised soreness.

"Huh," I muttered, for once at a loss for words.

Logan took it in stride. "Well. Now that I know Tania isn't at death's door," he said, peering around Birke to his sister's prone figure, "what's going to happen to her?"

Birke turned to gaze down at her. "She's going to sleep until she's fit to rule. Which, I have a strong suspicion, will be never. The real question is," she continued, turning back to scrutinize Logan, "who will rule in her stead?"

Logan shook his head, hands up. "Not me. I never had a taste for politics and I certainly don't now."

Birke nodded. "I suspected as much. I have a proposal. Would you like to discuss it?" She gestured to the side of the stage, indicating they should talk in private.

I stared at Gwyneira asleep on the ground. My reverie was interrupted by someone tugging at my hand.

"Tania?"

I turned, startled. Alejandro was standing by my side, blinking as though he'd just woken up from a long nap.

"Where are we? What happened?" He stuck his head around me and pointed. "Who's that lady, and why is she sleeping on the ground?"

I had no idea what to say. "It's, uh, a long story, kiddo, but we'll be home soon, okay?" Behind him, the other kids were milling around, all in similar states of sleepy confusion. Meanwhile, Birke and Logan seemed to have reached the end of their discussion and were walking back over.

As they drew near, some brave soul from the crowd walked forward, yelling, "Excuse me!" He wilted under Birke's unnerving gaze. "I, er, well, we were just wondering what's the conclusion of the duel?" He glanced from Gwyneira to us. "Who is the ruler now? And what are their policies?"

We all looked at each other. Logan nodded at Birke, and she bowed her head to him, then turned and strode toward the crowd, head held high with authority. "May I have your attention, please!" The crowd hushed at once, staring at the woman with the yellow eyes and pointy teeth. "Some of you know who I am. Some of you don't. That does not matter, because what *is* important is that I am now the ruler of this land." The crowd immediately started chattering. Birke silenced them with a wave of her hand. She pointed at Logan behind her. "The rightful ruler has bequeathed it to me, as he no longer wishes to have a part in it. As the new ruler, I have this to say: the children of the other world are under *my* protection. Anyone who continues to kidnap them will have to deal with me." She paused to smile slowly, showing each and every glinting, knifelike tooth. "Are we understood?"

Most of the people I could see in the crowd nodded and several backed up. I didn't think any of them were going to break any rules anytime soon. Couldn't say I blamed them—I wouldn't want to cross her, either.

"One last thing," she called out. "All current guards are dismissed, as I have no need for them. That is all, you may go." She walked back to us as the crowd started to disperse.

"So, Birke." I gestured to my stomach. "Am I always going to be impervious to stab wounds? Because that could come in handy."

She shook her head. "It's not meant to be permanent. In most cases, I undo it within a day or two." Her face grew somber. "But I can tell you'll need it for many days to come. Consider it a gift, until such a time as you don't need it any-more."

*That* was ominous as all get out. But still, no need to be rude. I half bowed and said, "I appreciate it."

Birke nodded, then turned to Logan. "Do you need any assistance with healing your injuries?"

He grimaced as he shook his head. "No, thank you. No of-fense, but I don't think I need to be in your debt."

She shrugged. "Suit yourself."

I glanced at the children, who were now gathered in a cluster, talking and looking around.

Birke followed my look. "I think it is time we take the chil-dren home."

"Okay, guys," I said to the gaggle of kids. "We'll have you home before too long. We'll just have to . . . walk a lot first."

Birke snorted. "This castle is now part of my lands, re-member? No need to make the children suffer more than they already have."

"Oh, you mean we can do the zoom-teleport-thing?" That was good news. Birke lifted a confused eyebrow at me, so I elaborated. "The thing that almost made me barf? How we traveled before?"

"Oh. Yes, we will travel my way." She spoke louder to the group of kids. "Children! Come here." They gathered around us, still staring around in a daze. "I want you all to hold hands. Can you do that for me?" They complied. Whatever mojo Gwyneira and her goons had put them under probably would take a while to wear off. Birke looked at Logan and me. We glanced at each other and clasped hands, then grabbed a child's hand on either side of us.

"Okay, guys," I told the kids, "hang on, it only takes a—"

Whoosh. Lurch. Just barely refrained from faceplanting. "Second," I finished as we all stood in a forest clearing. They took it remarkably well, examining their new surroundings with pleased surprise. It was a little easier on my stomach this time, and—thank heaven for small miracles—none of the kids ralphed.

And there, shimmering a few feet above the forest floor, was the Slip. I turned to Birke. "Thank you so much for all your help. I'll be back as soon as I can."

"I can reach you if I need to," she said.

I wasn't even going to ask what she meant by that. I was too tired for questions.

Logan bowed his head. "I echo Tania's thanks. We couldn't have done this without you. I appreciate that you repaid your debt in such a generous way."

Birke smiled at him and inclined her head in return. "Certainly. I have no doubt we will meet again." And with that, she was gone, nothing left except footprints in the snow.

I hesitated. Before we went home, I had one more question for Logan. "Do you want to stay here, Logan? Now that you're not banished? I would understand if you do . . ."

He looked around, staring at the magnificent trees and the

sun twinkling through the icy branches. I didn't know what he was going to say. It would make sense if he didn't want to come back with me, but I'd be sad nonetheless. After a minute or two of silence that stretched for ages, my heart in my throat, he shook his head.

"I don't think so. Now that I've faced her, I don't think much is left for me here. The only family I have"—he winked—"is over there. Unless . . . do *you* want to stay?"

That was something I hadn't considered. "I . . . I don't know. The idea has merit, I have to admit. It would be nice to train more." I sighed. "And to not be shut up in crappy apartment complexes, segregated from the rest of society." I laughed halfheartedly. "Then again, you guys don't have internal plumbing here. That's a pretty big deal."

Logan smiled, watching me, waiting for me to make a decision. "Well, let's get these kids home first, and then once we're back and I've cleared my name, maybe we can just duck back over." I shrugged. "Having a few normal weeks might help me decide."

He nodded. "Whatever you decide, I'm with you."

I grinned. "Careful, Logan. You keep talking like that and I'll think you've gone soft."

He punched me on the arm, laughing. "You're right. That's enough sentimentality for one day. Let's get these little snot-rockets home before they get hypothermia."

"All right, kids!" I shouted. The children, who had all stayed close, were starting to shiver. Grabbing Alejandro's hand, I continued, "Let's go home. Just follow me, okay? I promise it's not as scary as it looks."

I'd expected more resistance, or maybe fear. Whether it was the lingering effects of hypnosis or children's unquestioning acceptance of oddness, they lined up neat as a row of ducks.

We made it through the Slip with the familiar suspended, tingling feeling. And, with a gasp, we were back inside the lab. The children yelled in delight. I looked at Logan and squeezed his hand, beaming. "We did it, Logan. We actually pulled it off!"

He smiled back at my delight. Not a second later, his smile turned to horror, his eyes locked on something over my shoulder.

Before I could turn to see what he was looking at, I heard a *bzzt*, stars sparked across my vision, and everything went black.

My surroundings came into focus slowly, as though I was waking up with a killer hangover. I was . . . back in Birke's cabin? The fire was dying, the only light coming through the window, lining everything in silver. Outside, I could see the moon had finally started to wane.

Everything felt a little fuzzy around the edges. Not quite real. I walked to the fire to see if I could stoke it and bring more warmth into the room. As I bent over it, the door creaked, and I spun around, hoping Birke would have some answers.

Talk about a sight for sore eyes. Her apron was soaked in blood and bits of fur, and rust-colored stains ringed her mouth. With one hand, as though it weighed no more than a sack of potatoes, she was hauling a deer carcass by the scruff of its neck. She took no notice of me standing by the fire with my mouth agape.

"Birke, what the hell is going on? I was with Logan and the kids, then suddenly I'm back here." I waved my hands around for emphasis.

Dropping the deer with a thud, she turned to look around the cabin, eyebrows knit together. "Who's there? I'm in no mood for games, I warn you."

Like anyone would try to play a practical joke on a blood-covered witch. "It's me, Tania. I'm right here." I jumped up and down, waving my arms.

Her eyes slid right over me, then refocused, squinting. Taking a few steps closer, she said, "Tania? Is that you?"

I snorted, fed up with this game. "Who else would it be?"

Birke came closer still, reaching out a bloody hand to touch my face. I jerked away instinctively, grossed out by the blood, but it didn't matter—her hand brushed right through me, creating a weird tingling in my shoulder. *That* I was not expecting. In a week of supremely weird incidents, this was up there, and I was starting to get nervous. "Seriously, what's going on?"

"Tania, I can't make out what you're trying to say. I don't think you're strong enough to project your voice yet. But if you're here, like this . . . your life may be in jeopardy. I can't help you where you are. Stay on your guard. Keep pushing yourself and testing your skills. And remember, you're one of Mine now." She pressed her red fingertips to my forehead, through my forehead, and the room blurred again.

Gasping, I sat up with a start. My body ached all over, as though I'd been beaten. Everything around me was a glaring, sterile white—the cot I'd passed out on, the tiles, the hospital gown, the walls.

"Birke?"

No answer.

"Logan? Alejandro? Anyone? Somebody please tell me what's going on!" Trying not to panic, I walked over to the dull silver-colored door, the one thing that wasn't bright white. Pressing my hand against it, I balanced myself to get a better look through the window. Not a second later, I jerked away, swearing from the pain as my palm reddened from the iron. Standing on my tiptoes, I peered through the window, but all I could see was a hallway with more gleaming tiles, stretching off in either direction.

# ACKNOWLEDGEMENTS AND JAZZ

**Well, that's less than ideal, isn't it?** Don't worry, I'm working on getting book two done as fast as possible, so you can find out what the fried cheesesticks is going on and see what happens next. If you want updates, character sketches, behind the scenes notes, and other jazz, head over to *www.worldslip.net* to stay in the loop.

I've never written an acknowledgements list before, and at the end of this exhausting two-year journey, I feel like maybe I should have written one at the beginning, but I'm certain it would have changed by now. **So, here's a by-no-means exhaustive list of everyone I would like to thank for helping make this happen:**

Coni, Shenee, Alexis, Joey, and Ashley for alternately cheering me on, reading the first draft a chapter at a time and asking for the next chapter when it had been too long between them, and generally drowning out the loud sounds of self-doubt that come with doing any project that takes more than a year of your life. (Joey: sorry you're just now getting to read any of it. Hope it was worth the wait!)

Everyone else who cheered me on via Facebook, Twitter, and actual in-person interaction. Seriously, every single one of you. If you're thinking I forgot you, I didn't. I promise;. I just cannot list all the names here or this would go on for days. <3

My family for being supportive of my creativity and weird ambitions from childhood to now, even when I was a really obnoxious teenager.

The teachers who encouraged me, including but not limited to Mr. Turner and Mrs. Price-Allison. Kamila Forson for being a badass, supportive editor. And of course, you, for actu ally paying money for this and then reading it through to the literal end! (Insert introspective spiel about how I've wanted to be a writer since I could hold a pencil and this is the fulfillment of a lifelong dream, and you helped me do that, etc.)

That's not adequate, but I think it's the best I can do for now. Thanks for your love and support, I love you right back, thank you for reading, and stay tuned for book two, because there are many more wacky hijinks on the way!